Praise for C

"A hot, swe
-The Jorge Journal

"A swirl of fantasy in the head…"
-The Ahn Juno Times

"Four stars and a thousand pounds of star dust!"
-The Han Handout

"Ever since reading it, this book has filled my dreams."
-A Squeaker's Story Times

"Mysterious and well-written—a must read for all Koreans!"
-The Weekly Willy

"Like an addictive computer game, once you start reading, you can't stop!"
-The Sang Eon Review

"It'll make your hair stand up on end!"
-Sang Wong of the Daily Horn

"Similar to the Ember series and Wizard of Oz—but better!"
-The Min Young News

"I need his picture!"
-Squeaker's brother…again!

Copyright © 2015 by Tim Learn. All rights reserved.

Print Edition, License Notes
This book is licensed for your personal enjoyment only. This book may not be re-sold or given away to other people. If you would like to share this book with another person, please purchase an additional copy for each recipient. If you're reading this book and did not purchase it, or it was not purchased for your use only, then please return to your favorite book retailer and purchase your own copy. Thank you for respecting the hard work of this author.

Chewy Noh
and
the March of Death

To J.J. Byun
Sadly, the Chewy to my Clint

Prologue

The old man in the hospital bed tried once again to hold back his frustration, feeling briefly that maybe this was all payback, some kind of karma falling back upon him.

"It's unfair!" he said to the man at the window who waved a hand without looking over.

"It's the only way," the dark man responded, staring out over the land of bare, bony trees and gaunt, black birds.

The old man crossed his arms, huffing loudly. "You entice me with the boy and then say I can't even kill him!"

The dark man finally turned from the window with a calm smirk. His suit, an immaculate black sheen, would have shimmered were there any sun.

"There are extenuating circumstances that you

aren't aware of," the dark man said in monotone. His moustache lay flat above two pale lips.

"Like what?"

The dark man rubbed his forehead. If this was out of grief, the old man didn't know.

"Like that fact that there are ways around death. Just because you kill him, doesn't mean he'll stay dead."

The old man wrinkled up his face. What was this guy yammering on about? Death was the one thing everyone proclaimed as a certainty, and now this guy was saying otherwise.

"If that's so, why not do the same for me? Bring me back from the dead," he responded, pulling his blanket up over his ribs.

"Even if I kept you alive, it would never restore your body. It's too far gone for what I have in mind," the dark figure continued, raising a finger. "Besides, you'll see, being a specter has its advantages."

The old man wrinkled his brow at this. He had read enough when he was younger. He remembered a play where the devil came with promises but ultimately left with one's soul.

"Doesn't sound very reliable," he snorted.

"Your worries are justified, old timer. But if you follow my instructions, the boy will end up right where you're going, and if it's revenge you want, you'll have an eternity to administer it."

The old man's face twisted into a grin at this prospect, but soon the same concern crossed his mind again.

"How do I know any of this is true?" he snapped. The man had been in a coma for years. Many dreams had played him a fool.

"You don't," the dark man responded, returning to his chair against the wall. "But back where I come from, there is a large book. In it is the date of every person's death down to the second."

He paused, pointing to the clock above his head, and continued, "Your time is about to come up in exactly one hour. If you don't agree to my offer, a very ruthless creature will come for you. He is of a race that deals with the normal riff-raff, and he's right outside if you'd like to meet him. Ones like him enjoy hospitals."

He stretched a slender arm to the door, and the old man wrinkled his face up at this, causing the dark man to grin as he continued. "Here is what I can assure you: my friend outside will not make your death as pleasant as you may wish."

The old man shuddered, swallowing hard, and slowly nodded.

"Good," the dark man said. A smile grew beneath his thin, black moustache. He intertwined his fingers together before restarting. "In order to keep the boy down below, we'll need to take out the larger supports around him: his family, friends…his confidence."

With this last word, the old man's face lit up. He wanted that most of all, but the dark man raised his head to add more.

"You may want petty little revenge, but it will all fall apart if we're not careful."

The old man furrowed his brow. "Why don't you just kill these other…supports and leave him for me? Isn't that simpler?"

"I wish it were so," the dark man hummed. "Unfortunately, we gods cannot meddle so easily in human affairs. In some ways, we can push or redirect them, but in other ways our hands are quite tied. You see, the scope of a god's work is larger—a side effect of a much bigger playing field."

"So you're useless?"

A vicious grin spread over the mustached face sending a shiver up the old man's spine.

"On the contrary," he hissed, "I am allowed to kill only when that person has naturally expired or…if they've overstepped their bounds."

"What the hell does that mean?"

The dark man leaned forward. "That means if you follow what I say exactly, the boy will have no one to turn to, no one in his corner. And with that, not just him, but his whole family line will come to an end—much like yours has."

The rage flooded back into the old man's eyes. That old fool, Joong Bum, deserved as much. There was no turning back now. Wiping them out completely was the only option.

"So what do I have to do?"

The dark man tilted his head up for the old man to see his yellow eyes.

"Simple. Get the boy alone, make sure he has no other opportunity to escape you and," he raised a finger dragging it beneath his nose, "cut his philtrum. After that, I will do the rest."

Part I: Earth

1
My Grandfather and His House

-Joong Bum-

Hitting a bump, the bus rocked its passengers around, and nudged Joong Bum awake. He had dozed off for a second or two. Feeling the cold of the window with his hand, he wiped away the steam. Outside, the sky was dark, and in the distance, a full moon hung between mountain peaks. His mind was still in another world as he tried to figure out where he was.

He thrust his hands into his pockets for his phone, but didn't find it, and he furrowed his brow, realizing it was still on the kitchen table back at home. He had been in a rush, and as everything came back to him, he was left wondering how long he had slept. At the least, he hoped he hadn't missed his stop.

A road sign flying by put him at ease. He would be there soon, but he still felt stupid for forgetting his phone. What if there was trouble?

Two hours earlier, he picked up the phone,

thinking nothing special was in store, only to hear Yu-mi's voice. She apologized for calling so late, but he brushed it aside. After all, they hadn't spoken in years, but she sounded bothered, and he pressed her to speak.

"It's been the third night in a row now, and I just had to see how you were doing?"

He wrinkled his brow, staring out the glass of the veranda of his daughter's apartment into the night sky.

"I'm fine," he said, hesitating. "Third night of what?"

She answered slowly.

"I figured as much," she began. "My instincts are never wrong."

"How so?" he questioned. He knew she tended to be a bit superstitious, but for a woman who was going on eighty, maybe she knew some things others didn't.

"Your old place," she started again, "it's been dark for the past thirty years until two nights ago."

Joong Bum froze. She was talking about his parents' house. After his daughter was born, he moved to the city, leasing the country home out to whoever wanted it. But there were few takers for living that far out of society.

He quickly thanked her for the information and promised he'd be out to visit her personally soon. Immediately after hanging up, he changed into warmer clothes and left, leaving his phone on the kitchen table. His mind was elsewhere.

The bus churned to a halt, echoing in the dark night, and Joong Bum got off, finding himself on an old country road. The only light came from the lamp above the bus stop. The rest of the world was draped in shadows with skeletal branches scratching an ocean-colored sky.

Joong Bum had forgotten what the country was like. He had adapted greatly to his city life. Out here, everything was so clear. Even the air tasted different. He breathed in strongly and started heading down the old path home. It wasn't hard. He could still remember it from childhood and the days coming home from factory work, before Sae-rim had left.

He remembered a summer a long time ago when he was roughly fifteen. His older brother, Han Joong, and he were in front of their house tossing a baseball back and forth. Joong Bum wasn't particularly good at sports and envied his older brother greatly.

"You believe what they're saying?" Joong Bum asked. Han Joong also seemed a thousand times wiser.

Han Joong shook his head with a skeptical look to his eye.

"Don't believe everything you hear, little brother," he started with a snort. "Why would they come down here?" He paused a moment catching a wild throw, adding, "Besides, if the North is attacking us, that's way up by Seoul. It's not likely they'll make it down this far."

Joong Bum smiled. If his brother said it, then it must be true, and he stuck his glove out for the next toss.

After a high lob, Joong Bum heard the tinkle of metal from behind and turned to see the woman from the hill pass by on her bike. She waved to them and Joong Bum could tell the wave was mostly aimed at Han Joong. He was the handsome one, the one girls all liked, even older ones.

Joong Bum grimaced a little, tossing the ball lightly back to his brother who leaned over to catch the weak pitch. He would never be like his brother, and at times, it bothered him, but only with other people. When it was just him and Han Joong, everything was perfect.

"How are you taking to school?" his brother said, sending another high and soft toss.

Joong Bum didn't know how to answer. Since the Japanese left, it took a while for schools to pick up again, and Joong Bum didn't particularly like it. He felt he missed too much to understand what was going on. Besides, out in the country, what did he need an education for? They were rice farmers.

To answer his brother's question, he shrugged and in that second, caught a low hum he knew well. Turning back to the road, he saw Sae-rim, their second closest neighbor, skipping by. Her black hair shimmered in the sun and her round cheeks seemed to bulge with every step.

Seeing them, Sae-rim stopped for a second to

wave.

"Hello, Han Joong," her little voice squeaked. Joong Bum waved back but got no recognition as she continued on her way. Joong Bum's face turned a deep red. *Even Sae-rim!* Nobody paid attention to him, and he zipped around letting the ball fly without looking.

His brain was so flustered he didn't even notice the ball flew at their house. Han Joong dove to block it, but it was too late. The ball crashed through their front window. Within seconds, a loud bellow rang out from within, and out stomped their father. His face was as red as Joong Bum's had been just a second ago.

"Who?" their father yelled.

Joong Bum swallowed hard, staring at his father's throbbing eyes. But it was Han Joong who spoke first.

"I did it."

Their father tossed his eyes over the ground and picked up a stick. He then marched over to Han Joong, asking for his hands. Han Joong clenched his teeth and stuck them out, palms to the sky. Their father leaned in and swung mercilessly until the stick broke. Joong Bum couldn't watch and turned his back to the scene.

The old Joong Bum lowered his head trying to push the old memory behind him.

But that was a long time ago, and now there was someone in his parents' old house. True, it could just be a squatter looking for an abandoned, old place to call their own. Deep down, he knew better, but only one name kept rising up inside him—and that was impossible. For that person to be here, he would have had to cross many difficulties. He shook his head again.

Turning the corner, he caught the glowing house. He looked in the opposite direction, seeing Yu-mi's shack shining on top of a far off hill. For over eighty, she sure had amazing eyesight.

He took the path slowly and his heart beat faster. He was hoping to have figured out some kind of plan by now, but still his head was empty. The best thing he could do was just go and see.

Coming to the front porch, he heard movements inside and he pushed up to the door, pulling it open. The light poured out, illuminating the dead grass behind him, and he realized he was wrong. This wasn't the person he was expecting. Nonetheless, the visitor had traveled a long way.

But, how was this possible? Besides himself, no one really knew about the old house, not even his daughter—how did this person find it?

Clearly, Joong Bum expected an explanation. What he didn't expect was that upon entering his parents' old house, it would be another two weeks before he found his way out.

2
Our Second Meeting

-Chewy-

Chewy lifted his head to the dark room. He could have sworn he heard something and instinctively glanced at the spare bed opposite his. Ever since building a door bridge between their two rooms, Chewy routinely found his best friend, Clint, sleeping there. A run-in with a ghost could do that, and knowing this house was spiritually protected also helped. After tonight though, this would no longer be the case.

The bed was empty and Chewy turned back to his pillow happy. He wasn't in the mood to see Clint anyways—not after what he did. And it was then that he spotted the silhouette of a person in his withdrawn desk chair.

Believing he knew who it was, he ventured a "Grandma?"

The figure shuffled, coughing, and Chewy caught the distinct clack of leather against metal.

In that moment, the clear image of an old-style Korean soldier in full regalia stood out before him, and looking up, he saw a pair of eyes glow in the moonlight.

"Good evening, Mr. Noh," a deep voice said.

This was definitely not his grandmother. Chewy kicked at the sheets, pushing himself up against the head of the bed. He calculated whether or not he could make it to the bedroom door. If through it, he would be in the protection of the door bridge, but that meant getting past this shadow first. Through all of this, the man didn't move or speak until he saw Chewy was settled.

"Please," he started, holding up a thickly gloved hand, "I'm here merely for diplomatic purposes. For this reason, I'm allowed to pass through your mother's protections. I cannot hurt you."

Chewy lowered his arms, sitting more at ease. There was something about his deep voice, something genuine that resonated with Chewy. He felt he could trust this man.

"Who are you then?"

The man shifted again. Chewy easily imagined the full solider costume weighed immensely. There was no way it could be comfortable.

"Ah, yes, it's dark here," he said, turning his head around the room. "You'll have to forgive me. We run on Korean time and it's supposed to be day out."

He reached forward, finding the switch to the lamp on the desk. The light flicked on, and Chewy looked up to a well-trimmed goatee below powerful, piercing eyes. It took Chewy a second, but eventually, he knew who he was staring at.

"Gangnim."

The man appeared shocked for a second at Chewy's reaction before bowing his head.

Chewy recollected stories from his grandfather about this man, how the god of death, Yeomra, tricked him into becoming his messenger. Something inside Chewy went out to him, despite knowing this man was dangerous.

"So you're here to kill me," Chewy continued calmly.

A small, toothless grin appeared within the goatee.

"Not exactly," the man started, shifting his legs. "I'm here because of that."

He pointed to the scar below Chewy's nose. Chewy instinctively covered it. It no longer hurt, but he felt the tightness whenever he smiled, and he didn't like being reminded of what it stood for.

"Your grandmother worked hard to hide you from me, but eventually I found you. I must tell you then, that in a short time, I will return for you."

Chewy lifted an eyebrow. "So you came tonight to tell me that you're *going* to kill me?"

Gangnim lowered his eyes for a second in thought. "I've been doing this job for over a million years. The rules have changed a lot, mind you. In the beginning, I only had to address the mayor of a town before I took someone. You must understand, this was back when the world had much less people. Nowadays, there's just no time to follow these formalities. Most of the time, we don't even hand out warnings anymore. You're a special case, though."

Chewy's head twitched in recognition. A ghost had said the same thing to him recently and its meaning worried him. Hearing it again could be nothing good, and he kept his senses sharp.

"How so?" Chewy asked.

Gangnim set a gloved hand on the desktop before answering.

"Like I said, the population has increased. With it, I was given the task of handling the special cases. Normal footmen carry out the everyday duties," he said, lowering his head. "My job is to find the ones hiding from death—the ones purposely avoiding his decree."

"You mean I'm not the only one?"

Gangnim laughed, and the light from the desk painted deep shadows around his eyes.

"Lord, no," he said, putting his hand up to control his own laughter. "My hardest case was chasing a man named Samani. Like all areas of Korean life, corruption was rife, and this man was able to escape death the first time by bribing one of my elite officers. Afterwards, he eluded us for forty thousand years. He was a wily one, much like you."

Chewy took it as a compliment, his eyes

disappearing in a grin, and said, "Then how did you catch him?"

"My master is Yeomra, a god famous for his tricks, which means I, too, have picked up some of his habits over the ages. I went to a river and began washing a piece of charcoal. When people asked, I told them I had heard if you washed it for a hundred years, it would eventually become white. Not too long after, a man laughed at me, saying, 'I've been alive long enough to know the rock you hold will never turn white.' And with that I found my man."

"It was you then, wasn't it?" Chewy said, studying the man closely.

Gangnim tilted his head. "Me?"

"In order to catch me, you sent that ghost to give me this scar. He said as much, mentioning I was special, just like you did now."

To this, Gangnim lowered his eyebrows. Clearly, this was news to him as well.

"I'm sorry," he said, looking deeply into Chewy's eyes. "But that I don't know."

"Then what happens next?"

Gangnim's lips went flat, and a grim look came to his penetrating eyes.

"I advise you to get your things in order. Say your good-byes," he said, his eyes dropping upon Chewy's face. "In one week's time, Mr. Noh, you will be dead."

3
When I was still Great

-Chewy-

After his middle of the night chat, it took Chewy two days to figure out what to do. If anything, the little story of the man who cheated death was an inspiration, just what he needed at that moment. His life had not been going particularly well up to that point. Above all, it distracted him from a much heavier event.

While waiting for his so-called best friend to come across the door bridge, Chewy reviewed over the past two weeks, looking out his bedroom window. The warm March sunlight had turned every sidewalk and open area into a festival of mud and slush. It was a further reminder that he hadn't been outside at all—this included school. His mom was afraid the scar would bring danger. And she was right.

Two weeks earlier, the ghost that was out for revenge gave him that scar. Being stuck in a door bridge with the specter, Chewy came up with a plan to trap it there, unaware that only the person imbued with the spirit of the mu-dang could remove the bridge's incantation. Before exiting the bridge, his face exploded in pain, and the scar stood as a constant reminder of a failure he desperately wanted to forget.

And now there was a deadline. He just hoped this failure didn't hang over him for too long.

Before he could get too entrenched in this thought, Clint burst through the door with Chewy's pile of missed homework. Chewy turned to him with a flat mouth. He wanted his friend to know immediately that nothing had changed.

Clint paused mid-room, his eyebrows uplifted. "You still angry?"

Chewy's face stayed frozen.

"What do you think?" he said.

Earlier that week, Clint admitted to using Chewy's missing power to his advantage in order to get the upper hand in every argument and activity they did together.

"Needless to say," Chewy remarked, lowering his voice "no more Rock, Scissors, Paper."

He had lost a record ninety-eight in a row.

"I told you it was a stupid way to make decisions," Clint mumbled, lowering his head to look weak.

Chewy knew it wasn't solely Clint's fault. He too had gotten used to the easiness his life was with the power. Only afterwards, did he realize it affected other aspects than getting A's on tests.

Beforehand, anytime he went to watch TV, his favorite shows and movies were on. Now, there always seemed to be dramas about girls crying over their cats or not getting enough roses or something. It was rather frustrating, but that didn't mean his best friend was supposed to use it against him—especially to just get pineapple on his pizza.

Chewy turned to him, imagining a suitable revenge when Clint jumped in.

"You'll never guess what happened in school today," he said, waiting long enough to grab Chewy's attention. "After lunch, Kent was pushing some fourth grader into the slush outside. I think he wanted to show the school he was back in charge now that you're gone."

Chewy looked up. Compounded with his other problems, he realized he had far too many enemies for not even being a teenager yet. He was happy, though, as it seemed he was off Kent's radar for the time being.

"A lot of people are beginning to believe you're never coming back," Clint said sadly, pausing to show he was among them. "Anyways, before anyone knew it, Kent missed the kid and slipped on leftover ice or snow or something. The point is he ended up breaking his arm. He's going to come to school on Monday with a whole cast and everything."

Chewy's eyes opened wide. Maybe his luck wasn't all bad nowadays. Something was paying Kent back for all the harassment he'd done—the least of which was trying to burn Chewy alive and kick him out of school for cheating. And then something popped into his head.

"He had an accident?"

Clint shrugged, saying, "Yes."

"But with his power to always be better than me, you'd expect that wouldn't happen. I mean I can't ever recall having an accident until recently."

Chewy had more stubbed toes than he could count lately. In fact, he was pretty sure he had fully reverted back to the old Chewy—the way he was before ever getting that wish up in the mountain. No more perfect tests. No more luck—on anything. And this got Chewy back on track.

"Something's happened," he declared.

Clint understood immediately they were no longer talking about their fight or Kent, and he looked at Chewy with his classic worried face. Chewy couldn't help but smile.

"I've thought a lot about it and I feel it's time we did something about this," Chewy said, spinning a finger in a circle to insinuate his confinement.

Clint plopped down on the guest bed. "I'm afraid to ask," he said, setting his hands atop his leg braces.

"Then it's probably best if you didn't," Chewy said, looking to the bed Clint sat upon. It had been his cousin, Su Bin's until she went back to Korea. He already missed her and knew his best friend felt the same. Though Clint would never admit it—there was something going on between the two.

If Chewy was going to move forward, he knew he would need her help as well. With his smart power gone, she was the next best thing, and besides, he needed someone who could also speak Korean. Clint was far behind in that subject, with or without his crush.

He went over and put a hand on his friend's shoulder, forgetting his anger for the time being.

"All you need to know is you're sleeping over tonight like usual. And I promise, by tomorrow morning, you will be asking yourself, 'How did the great Chewy Noh do it again?'"

Clint's eyes went dull. "I highly doubt that."

In the end, Chewy was right. On top of it, he was able to slip in a little bit of payback as well.

4
Burning Bridges

-Clint-

Normally, Clint slept on his back, sprawled out. It was easier on his legs. Whenever he lay on his side, his knees started aching, and his legs lost all feeling due to his braces. He hated that.

So a little after midnight, when he heard Chewy's door shut, he opened his eyes immediately with a clear view of the room. Without lifting his head, he caught two figures inching toward him. He didn't know why, but something inside him didn't like it.

He sprang upright in bed to warn Chewy, but a hand slipped over his mouth before he could even get a word out. Even if he had wanted to scream, his voice went dead in his throat.

He was beginning to think that maybe Chewy was right. They had to do something except now it seemed they were a little bit too late. The other shadow reached out, flicking on the lamp, and Clint squirmed, squinting as his eyes adjusted.

What he saw was unexpected.

Su Bin's face glowed three inches away from his with a ridiculously large smile. Her eyes were hidden in two curvy lines. Looking over to the desk, Clint saw the same face on Chewy. For a second, he was unsure whether it was due to the shock of everything or the fact that Su Bin was touching him, but he realized his heart was beating like mad.

"Don't get too comfortable," she said with a giggle. "That's my bed."

She pulled her hand away as Clint tossed his head between both of them and squeaked out a "why" in between breaths.

Chewy just stood there with a proud smirk. His arms were crossed as if satisfied with himself, and Clint gulped. Was all of this on purpose? He looked to Su Bin's tiny eyes. Well, if it was, at least, there seemed to be an upside to it, and he watched her take a seat at the edge of his bed.

Eventually, the awe of seeing her again and having her touch him wore off, and the use of his voice came back to him. "How?"

Chewy flopped down on his bed, legs dangling over the edge. "You believe this guy? Out before ten o'clock—at a sleepover! Lucky nothing's trying to kill him."

"Hey, I'm right here," Clint said, setting his feet on the floor. "Now, is someone going to answer me?"

He looked to Su Bin, and seeing her shocked

expression, squeaked out a "please" to soften his demand.

"Relax," Chewy said, waving a hand. "While you were snoring, I made a door bridge from my closet to Su Bin's. Figured it might come in handy in the future."

Clint slowly rotated his head over to Su Bin's beaming face. He was now only two doors away from where she slept.

On the other side of the room, Chewy sat up straight, glaring, and Clint froze. How did he still do that without his power? Clint quickly spat out a concern to throw off Chewy's disapproving stare.

"I love seeing Su Bin and all," he started, noticing her bashful, lowered head at this comment, "but it's not like you're about to jump back to Korea and start walking around. You don't even know what's trying to kill you! And until you do, this house is the best place to be."

Finishing, Clint saw a look of confidence spread over Chewy's face. He wasn't looking forward to hearing what his friend had to say.

"Then lucky for us I know who's trying to kill me," Chewy said, pointing directly at Clint's shocked eyes.

Clint shook his head greatly. This was on purpose—all of it! Chewy never withheld important information like that just to make Clint look stupid, and Clint kicked himself. He should have known his little plan to abuse Chewy's missing power wasn't going to work, but there was no turning back now.

"That's even more of a reason not to go outside," Clint snapped.

"Where's the fun in that?" Chewy said, smiling.

Su Bin stared at both of them with a confused look on her face to which Chewy lifted a hand, saying, "Can you give us minute?"

He grabbed Clint from off the bed, led him over to the closet, and pulled Clint's head down so both were in ear-range of each other before starting to whisper.

"What is up with you?"

"What's up with you?" Clint echoed back. "You know it's not safe to go outside. You're just doing this because you're still mad at me."

"Of course, I am! You're my best friend! Why would you use me like that—when I'm at my weakest!"

Clint shook his head. Did Chewy really not see it?

"You've been number one since the day we met, so I know what it's like to always come in second place. I just thought maybe it would be good for you to do the same."

Chewy's eyes widened immensely. "You knew how my power worked. It's not like I did it on purpose!"

"Well, you sure seemed to enjoy it while you had it," Clint snapped back, and he saw Chewy's face flush. In that instant, he knew things were about to go too far.

"Alright then," Chewy started again, narrowing his eyes, "now that I don't have my power—let's just see who ends up on top."

And he swung back around to his cousin waiting patiently on the bed.

"I'm hungry!" Chewy announced. "You up for some duk-bok-ki?"

Su Bin's face lit up, and she turned to Clint, clearly wanting to see the same joy from him. So he faked a smile, all while a sinking fear rose in his stomach.

"That doesn't resolve the fact that something is out there trying to kill you—whether you know what it is or not," Clint said, hoping—all anger aside—reason would get through to him.

"Just give me time to explain. I swear it'll all make sense in the end. I promise you we have nothing to worry about, at least, for now," Chewy said, putting up his hands to look less offensive, but Clint could tell it was all an act as he continued, "Please, I can't do this without my best friend."

Clint quickly looked back to Su Bin who had her eyebrows up as if pleading with her large, round eyes. She came over placing a hand on Clint's shoulder. In that instant, his brain turned off. He could barely feel his toes.

"Please," she squeaked.

Clint batted his eyes trying to get his thoughts back. The only thing he did feel was that the whole situation was unfair. Chewy using his own cousin against him! Well, if that's the way he wanted to play, Clint could do it too! He placed his hand atop Su Bin's, and looked deeply into her face as she blushed.

"Alright, I'll go," he said.

Clint leaned over catching the stern glare from his best friend. Hopefully, Chewy knew whom he was dealing with now, and they could end this little game.

Heading for the closet door, Clint leaned over, whispering into Chewy's ear. "Duk-buk-ki—it's super spicy, isn't it?"

"I have no idea what you're talking about, buddy," Chewy said, placing a hand on Clint's shoulder as he went past. Clint was afraid of that.

"Would it help if I apologized?"

Without evening looking back, Chewy responded, "Not a chance."

For a second, Clint wished they had never woken him up, that two ghosts had attacked instead, until Su Bin turned her round face up to his at the closet door, grinning.

Chewy opened the door, revealing a thick darkness. Somewhere on the other end was Korea, and he marched in without hesitation. Before entering herself, Su Bin reached out, squeezing Clint's hand, and only one thought appeared in his head. *It couldn't be that spicy, right?*

5
I worry myself

-Chewy-

Clint coughed heavily, nearly falling off the plastic, red stool. He reached out blindly, slamming his fingers against the metal counter as Su Bin glided a cup of water into his hands. Chewy just stood there watching it all with a smile. Despite Clint's jealousy, Chewy was going to miss these times.

"It's really not that spicy," he muttered, turning back to his paper tray of rice cake drowned in red sauce.

In three months, school would be done for the year. That meant Chewy had to go back to Korea and leave Clint behind. He was a little worried that their friendship would dissolve. Why wouldn't it with all that space in between? That was partly why he had made a door bridge connecting the two countries, but he knew even that wouldn't necessarily stop their friendship from falling apart.

He popped another gooey rice cake in, feeling his mouth tingle. It had been so long it was as if he was eating them again for the first time.

Even though Chewy didn't fully understand why Clint was upset, if anything, their fight just proved how close they were. Clint wasn't like any of his other friends. And their fight seemed silly to Chewy at that moment only because it was his power that brought them together in the first place. That was one reason why Chewy felt Clint was special. Something much bigger made them friends, not just, "Hey, you and I have the same teacher," or "Wow, you live in the same gigantic apartment complex as I do!"

Clint had regained control of his mouth, and Chewy tossed a finger up to the old woman behind the counter, ordering a new entree.

But Chewy did have to admit, he was happy being back in Korea one last time. He looked up at the orange vinyl cover of the small street vendor's booth they huddled inside of. In front of them, steam rose from open vats of foggy water, presenting their skewers of fish cake and fried meat. His eyes floated over all of it, not knowing what to try next, and he grabbed the fried flat bread the vendor passed to him.

He then dropped it to Clint and said, "It's sweet inside. Don't worry."

Clint squinted, not knowing whether to trust Chewy or not, but he grabbed it anyways.

The sun beat in through the plastic tarp

windows. Korea was a full twelve hours or so ahead of time, so it was midday Saturday. It was also unbridling cold, and having forgotten to bring warmer clothes, both Clint and Chewy found themselves in borrowed jackets.

With Chewy and Su Bin being the same size, it wasn't so bad, but for Clint, it was a different story, and this only made Chewy smile more. He couldn't have planned it more perfectly, watching Clint on a small stool, shoving ho-duk into his mouth, his arms sticking out of a super-small, pink jacket. He wished his phone wasn't broken so as to take a picture.

He passed the old vendor some money for the bread and was glad she didn't know much English; otherwise, the conversation he had planned would be quite alarming to her. And he cleared his throat to get their attention.

"Two nights ago, Gangnim visited me."

Both knew well who Gangnim was and looked at him with furrowed brows.

"He gave me roughly one week to say my good-byes, and then he'd be coming for me."

Su Bin's face scrunched up in distress, and she extended a hand to Chewy's shoulder.

"There's gotta be something we can do," she said.

Clint nodded in agreement. For the time being, Chewy could see his friend had forgotten their differences.

"Can't your mom hide you?" Clint said.

Chewy shook his head and then pointed at his scar.

"Because of this, he can find me. If anything, my mom can hold him off, but…he is a professional. It's his job to find people who don't want to be found."

He related the story of Samani escaping death for forty thousand years. At the end, he noted to himself that he wouldn't have the same luck now that his power was gone. But he hid it from the others to keep up a strong appearance.

"So there's nothing we can do?" Su Bin said, her voice growing faint.

Chewy put his hand up to stop any tears. He knew, eventually, it'd be hard enough to keep his own back.

"There may just be a way," he said and could see the hope enter their eyes. "My grandmother sort of swore me to secrecy, but I don't think it matters much now."

He went on to tell them about how his grandfather had cursed the family by pretending to be his own brother—Chewy's grandmother's real husband—and that was the only reason Death was after him in the first place.

"So we just have to go break the curse," Su Bin announced.

Chewy smiled. He was beginning to see more and more of himself in her. She was no longer quite the perfect student he remembered only a couple months ago. Clint, on the other hand, was his normal worrisome, but logical self.

"If it were that easy, why hasn't your mom—or your grandmother for that matter—done the very same thing?" Clint asked.

Chewy breathed deeply before responding. "I don't know. But it looks like going to my grandfather may be the only option."

He saw Clint nod and Su Bin bow her head in understanding. They both knew Chewy was on his own. Before getting his scar, he had his grandmother for guidance, but now, with the threat of death hovering around him, Chewy's mom blamed his grandmother for all of it. He hadn't spoken to her since the night of the attack.

"I know she's still in there," he said, wondering how his mom was able to cut off all contact with a spirit she shared a body with. "Sometimes, I get flashes of things in my mind…which are supposedly her."

Clint jerked his head. "What do you mean?"

"She told me last month I was supposed to be the mu-dang—not my mom—but my grandfather messed it all up. Despite that, a little bit of her spirit got into me. Because of it, I can…see things from time to time."

"You mean read minds?" Su Bin squeaked.

"Sort of," Chewy said, scrunching up an eye. He caught Clint's frozen stare insinuating he now knew why Chewy could still guess when he was thinking of Su Bin.

"That's also why my mom probably wasn't

alerted to me making a door bridge tonight or us leaving the house. My grandmother must be in there messing with her thoughts."

"Then what are we waiting for?" Su Bin squeaked. "Let's go find your grandfather!"

Chewy's eyes began to water. This was the part he didn't know how to explain.

"I've already tried," he said, catching their surprised faces. "The past two weeks whenever my mom slipped out for groceries, I've tried using the home phone to get in touch with him. Every time I call, no one answers. He doesn't seem to be around."

Su Bin's eyes grew small before speaking again. "You think something's happened to him?"

Chewy shook his head, holding back his tears. "I don't know, but whatever it is, if we don't find him by next Wednesday, Gangnim will be back. And I'll be dead."

6
Showtime

-Chewy-

Chewy and Clint climbed back into their beds a little after five in the morning, sleeping until almost noon. Chewy's mom paid little notice. She had a full schedule of baby-namings and fortune-readings to deal with.

Besides sulking over some sweet bread, they spent the rest of the night figuring out what to do but came up with little. Su Bin would search on her end for Chewy's missing grandfather—it was the logical choice. And for Chewy, he had the job of telling his mom—something he wasn't looking forward to doing. Clint's job was to make sure Chewy did it.

They waited until midday Sunday to do so. And afterwards, clearly Clint was happy he was only one door away from home. Chewy's mom did not take the news well.

Otherwise, they were able to put the fighting behind them for the time being, but the tension was always there, festering under the surface. Whenever it came time to choose what to have for snack or what to watch on TV, a small bit of animosity rose between them. For now though, they kept it quiet. After all, if Chewy wasn't dead by Wednesday, they could always resume the challenge of topping the other one. Unfortunately, things changed faster than they ever imagined.

By the time Clint came charging over the door bridge after school on Monday, Chewy had a lot to share. He quickly raced Clint out to the bay window overlooking the front lawn and the street.

"You see that guy?" he said, pointing to a shadowy figure in a parked blue sedan that resembled something from out of the seventies.

Clint nodded, squinting.

"He's been there since this morning," Chewy said, slipping down behind the couch edge to stay hidden. "He never moves. Just sits there."

"You think it's Gangnim?"

"I think it's related. And I'm afraid to tell my mom about it." Chewy sank lower into the couch, staring blankly at the wall. Since the day before, his mom had gone overboard and he began detailing it all to Clint, pointing in different directions around the house.

"She's blessed the doors to stop any new bridges. Planted orange trees out front—supposedly it scares away death," he said, rolling his eyes. "And right now, she's out looking for metal pins like Samani had to hide from Death's radar."

"You really think any of this is going to work?" Clint said, slipping down onto the couch.

"There's more," he said, dropping his head. Chewy had saved the worst for last. "She's also renamed me."

He had spoken in a low voice but knew Clint heard it, catching his head turn slowly toward him with question marks in his eyes. Chewy cut him off before he could even start.

"It's actually not that uncommon," he said, holding his gaze on the floor. "In second grade, the kid next to me did it too. Said the fortune-teller thought his old name would make him poor and unsuccessful. He was particularly lousy in science."

Clint lifted an eyebrow. "And your name?"

"Well, it's not going to make me better at science if that's what you're asking," Chewy said, sticking out his lips at the absurdity of it.

"I meant what is it?" Clint corrected.

Chewy closed his eyes. For a second, he thought about lying, because, well, it's not like Clint would ever know the difference.

"Bo-mi," he spat out with eyes closed. Hearing silence, he opened them to see Clint shrug. "It may not mean anything to you, but it sounds exactly like the word for spring in Korean. I might die in two days and I still can't even have a cool, boy-sounding name."

Clint's head flipped around for a second to the

window and then paused. Chewy stared at him as he pointed toward the street.

"You'll never believe this," Clint said in a weak voice. "But I think that's Kent out there and he's hobbling this way."

Chewy spun back to the window, and Clint was right. Kent Grumbly was making his way, although with great difficulty, up Chewy's driveway. His right arm hung in a sling, his left ankle wrapped in bandages. Neither boy moved until he reached the front door and rang the bell.

"What do you think he wants?" Clint said.

"How should I know? I haven't seen him in weeks. I figured he had completely forgotten about me," Chewy responded, pausing as the bell rang again. "You think we should pretend no one's home?"

Clint lifted his eyebrows and shoulders as if to say "not a bad idea," but then Kent began shouting.

"Chewy! We need to talk—now!"

Chewy got up, heading for the door when Clint whispered after him, asking what he was doing.

"Answering the door," Chewy remarked in his normal tone, not wanting to hide anything. "I'll be dead in two days, so what can he do to me? Besides, kind of curious as to what he has to say, especially since he's deciding to call me by my normal name."

Clint jumped off the couch to stop him, but Chewy already had the door open, looking at a completely ravaged Kent. Besides his clearly visible injuries, Kent's eyes were red from what looked like missing sleep, and he had small cuts all over his hands.

Noticing Chewy's stare, Kent lifted his one good arm up for both to see. "More than a lifetime of paper cuts in just the past week."

Chewy cringed looking at it. He wanted to feel sorry for him. Even a monster like Kent didn't deserve what looked like torture. And he glanced back up at Kent's red-eyed face that was glaring at him as if looking for answers.

"What?" Chewy said, stepping a bit back from the door and felt Clint's hand on his back for support.

"Everyday, my clumsiness and bad luck seem to be getting worse," he said, his voice faltering slightly. "I figured if anyone knew why, it was you and your witch mom."

Chewy's eyebrows dropped.

"Sorry—no witches here," he said, shutting the door only to find Kent's one good foot blocking it.

"Alright! I'm sorry," Kent spit out. "But there's gotta be something you can do."

Chewy looked to Clint's worried face. He didn't even need his slight mind-reading ability to know which three words were flowing through Clint's head on repeat. *Don't do it!*

Chewy shook his head with a smile. How was he not supposed to do it now? He tossed the door open and waved Kent in, all in front of Clint's white, horrified face.

After Kent passed, Chewy glanced at the car across the street. The driver seat was now empty, and he shrugged. Maybe he was wrong. Maybe it had nothing to do with him, and he turned to Kent, closing the door.

"My mom's gone right now, but she should be back soon. You can wait in my room until then."

Kent nodded and then sniffed the air.

"What's that smell?" he said, wrinkling his face in disgust.

"That was lunch," Chewy started, "Kimchi soup. If it bothers you, you can always wait outside."

Chewy extended his arm back toward the front door, and Kent shook his head.

"Alright then," Chewy resumed. "My door's the first one on the left."

He and Clint watched Kent go down the hall, disappearing into Chewy's room. Within a second, Clint had Chewy by the sleeves.

"Are you crazy? What if he beats Gangnim to the punch and kills you before Wednesday? Maybe that's how death works?"

Chewy shook free of Clint's grip.

"I don't think so," Chewy said, wrinkling his brow. "He looks fairly genuine and pathetic. Besides, he's in my room. If he tries anything, we can just slip into the door bridge and he'll never be able to touch us."

The color still hadn't returned to Clint's face.

Chewy sighed. "What?"

"I can see your mom was wrong. Changing your name won't help at all," Clint said, squinting at Chewy. "Locking you in a closet would've been a better idea. Then I'd at least still have a best friend by next weekend."

Chewy scrunched up his face, waving away Clint's nonsense, and headed for his room with Clint trailing after.

With both of them gone, the kitchen lay silent until the refrigerator door broke it with a creak as it slid open. A cool breeze drifted out, followed by two large leather boots stretching their way to the linoleum floor below.

7
Unexpected Side Effects

-Clint-

Walking into the room, Clint and Chewy found Kent staring around as if in a foreign land.

"Why the hell do you have levers next to all your doors?" he asked, rubbing the shoulder his sling hung on.

Clint slipped over next to the closet to keep Kent at a maximum distance, and then he watched Chewy go over and drape himself on the bed. Clint couldn't believe he was being so relaxed about this.

"It's an old house," Chewy said, nonchalantly. "The doors jam sometimes."

Clint marveled at Chewy's bravado. He came up with the lie so naturally. Inside, Clint wished they could say otherwise. He had built them after all to open the doors from the other side so that they didn't get trapped in the room by the door bridges. But he could do little bragging about it without having to explain way too much more.

"Only you?" Chewy lazily drawled out from the bed.

"What do you mean?" Kent said, dropping his large eyebrows.

"Tom's fine—no injuries?"

"Of course not! Why do you think I'm here?" Kent said, holding his one good arm out. "That lummox has no idea."

With that, Clint forgot his anger, realizing something was going on here.

"You said this started about a week ago?" Clint glanced at Chewy who had lifted an eyebrow of interest.

"The major injuries…yes," Kent replied.

Clint squinted. It was all beginning to make sense. "Yes? So you had problems even earlier?"

Kent shoved out his lips. He didn't seem to trust either of them.

"Maybe," he opened with before deciding it'd be okay. "Like three weeks ago."

The test—that was it! It all started when Chewy had lost his power—well, not really lost it. Clint had to wish it away to save his best friend from expulsion for cheating, but he had a feeling it was somehow connected.

Clint began nodding causing Chewy to sit up in bed.

"What is it?" he asked.

"Don't you see? That was when everything started going downhill for you too," Clint said. "I think I understand what's going on now."

He smiled only to find the two other individuals in the room staring at him with questioning glares. He put up his hands to signal that he'd explain and moved into the middle of the room, feeling slightly braver.

"Kent wished to be better than you at everything. By doing that, his abilities became linked to yours. If you were the best, he was just a little better. But if you somehow ended up becoming the worst…" he trailed off, letting them connect the dots.

"Are you saying," Kent growled, pointing a strict finger at Chewy, "that because he now sucks, I suck too."

Chewy began giggling on his bed, drawing both of their attentions before he was able to squeak out his words.

"Close," he said, wiping away some tears. "But not exactly. I suck so you suck just a little bit less than me."

Chewy broke into a fit of giggles again, causing Kent to snap.

"Then what are you laughing at?"

Chewy swallowed hard to control himself. "Because it all makes sense now. Last week, right around when all your accidents started, I was informed that by this Wednesday I would be dead. And what's only slightly worse than that?"

Clint's face went flat with disbelief, but Chewy was right. What was one step better than dying—getting every bone broken? Being a walking calamity of accidents? If that were true, it seemed to say there was little either Clint or Chewy could do to stop the event on Wednesday from happening. And his anger began to rise thinking of Chewy's overwhelming confidence.

Before he could finish this thought, a thump rang out behind him.

Clint spun around, seeing a large man dressed in a billowing, black robe as if wearing a cape, and a broad black hat. After the ghost had attacked them earlier that winter, Chewy showed Clint many pictures of Korean spirits and ancient gods. This man looked eerily familiar like an old time solider complete to the last detail, including the shiny sword glinting in his right hand.

In a second, Clint's brain turned off, and he lunged for the door, slamming it shut. He heard his own voice yell out, "Chewy!" And then, he swung the door back open, revealing a long black corridor and dove in.

He hit the ground hard, staring down into a sea of black. For this reason, door bridges always freaked him out. It was like walking across an endless pit without falling. But he pushed all of this away, flipping over just in time to catch Chewy jumping on top of him.

Both screamed from the collision but quickly realized neither was injured. It was more so out of fear than pain. They scrambled to their knees and stared out the open door bridge at Kent who had turned white seeing both of them disappear right in front of a large Korean man.

The man stepped into the room, and Kent began throwing things aside—the desk chair, blankets and pillows—to get as far away as possible. His injuries, however, made it difficult, and he fell to the ground, slamming his already broken arm on the floor. The crack of the cast breaking made both Clint and Chewy cringe as they watched on.

Clint tried saying something but his voice didn't seem to work. Luckily, Chewy's did.

"Don't worry. He should be okay. Remember it's me they want."

Clint nodded, but this didn't seem to stop his heart from thrashing around inside. Then the man in the room shifted his head to the side, almost as if looking backward to where they were hidden. Clint knew the door bridge kept them out of sight, but it seemed like this specter wanted them to see something.

The man's eyes narrowed, and then he lifted the sword above Kent who was frozen in fear. Clint wished Kent would've made some kind of sound—anything—then maybe the man would leave.

At that moment, the soldier twisted his arm and drove the blade of his sword right through Kent's chest. Kent's head uplifted for a second as if to meet the thrust, and his eyes bulged either in pain or disbelief before collapsing to the floor. A moan escaped his body as it stopped moving.

Retracting his blade, the solider held the sword

up as if to admire it, holding it in clear sight for both of them to see. It had no blood, but Kent's body still wasn't moving. And the soldier turned toward them and walked out the door, leaving the room empty.

For the first few seconds, neither spoke, but just stared at Kent's lifeless body before Clint was able to muster enough of his voice back.

"How?"

Next to him, Chewy swallowed hard, his eyes focused on the body in front of them.

"I don't know," he said shaking his head. "I don't know."

8
I'm still in the dark

-Clint-

Chewy waited only a second before stepping out of the door bridge's protection, slinking over to Kent's unmoving body. Clint wasn't quite yet ready to do so, especially since the house no longer seemed safe.

Chewy twisted his head once or twice over the body, lowering himself to inspect it closer, and then he called out to Clint who still hovered in the door bridge.

"There seems to be no wound. No blood," he said, looking back at Clint. "You think he's really dead?"

Clint just stared. This couldn't be happening, and his brain was firing all over the place, shooting thoughts faster than he could even comprehend.

Kent coming made sense. His life was falling apart, but why today? And why did that soldier have to kill him? Something didn't seem right but

he couldn't wrap his head around it, and it frustrated him until his anger set in again. He looked up at Chewy who was clapping to get a reaction from Kent's unresponsive face.

"You just couldn't listen, could you?" Clint snapped, finally standing up.

Chewy lifted his eyes from Kent. "What are you talking about?"

Clint charged from the bridge, slamming the door shut. For all they knew the soldier was lurking in the house somewhere, but Clint couldn't hold it back any longer.

"If you hadn't let him in, none of this would've happened!"

Chewy's eyebrows lowered as he squinted at Clint's reddening face.

"You think I'm responsible for this?" Chewy said, pointing down at Kent.

"You just had to be curious and let him in. Sometimes I wonder what life would be like if you didn't just jump in whenever something pops up," said Clint, tossing his arms out. He felt like kicking something but found nothing besides Kent in range, and that probably wasn't going to help things.

Chewy moved closer, glaring up at him.

"Instead, you'd probably suggest what?—we go and hide, wait until it all just goes away, right?" Chewy snapped. "You think ignoring our problems would be better?"

That wasn't what Clint meant. He admired

Chewy's bravery, to defy what others said, except for when Chewy turned it on him. Sometimes, he thought it would have been better for Chewy to keep his power. Without it, his options looked bleak. It meant he would have to change as well.

"All I'm saying is that maybe we'd have one less dead body lying around."

Chewy's eyes grew wider than Clint had ever seen them.

"Do you think for a second that if we'd go back in time right now and stop me from letting Kent in that any of this would be different?" Chewy spit out in one breath before jumping right into the next one. "If it wasn't Kent, this may've been you. Then where would we be?"

Chewy lowered an eyebrow as if realizing something. "This is all about before," he said slowly. "You're still angry because you don't like coming in second place!"

Clint held a finger out at him. "Don't! Don't even start!"

"Start what?" Chewy said, backing away.

"Start getting in my head. Once you do, nothing makes sense." Clint turned his back, biting his lip. How could he get his best friend to understand what was bothering him? Chewy only ever saw the immediate; he was always just reacting to something. For once, he wished Chewy would say, "You know what—let's see it Clint's way." But he knew that would never happen because Chewy couldn't see his own faults. He only thought about coming out on top.

"Can't you see? I am not angry about you beating me," Clint blurted out with his back still turned. "That was never the problem. Being second to you was wonderful."

Chewy tilted his head, finally looking a bit out of sorts. "Then what?"

"When the ghost attacked us two weeks ago, and I went charging into the door bridge after you, I was afraid," he said, turning back to Chewy to hold up a finger as he saw Chewy open his mouth to speak. "Listen! I was afraid because you didn't have your power anymore, and I knew that no matter what, you were going to be the normal Chewy—running into things with half a plan. But you know what? That won't work anymore. The scar under your nose proves it! Your luck is gone and I wanted you to get used to it! So that maybe you'd…"

He trailed off, not noticing tears had come to his eyes. Seeing this, Chewy lowered his shoulders, the anger draining from his face.

"You weren't jealous," he said more in confusion than a question.

Clint nodded. He knew it was foolish. He always knew. How could a plan like that ever work—to teach your friend a lesson? If he had seen what losing was like, maybe he would see he would have to be more careful in the future. There was no more luck, and the last thing Clint wanted was to lose the only best friend he'd ever had.

Chewy put his hand on Clint's shoulder, startling him.

"We have a long road ahead of us—together," Chewy said as his own eyes welled up. "I promise you, this Wednesday will not be the last time you see me. Not if I can help it, at least. I swear."

This helped, and Clint felt a lot of the tension from the past couple weeks lift. He knew it wasn't permanent. What Chewy said didn't resolve the underlying issue of being honest to himself. But it showed Clint had made a chink in Chewy's rigid thinking. Now, Clint just hoped it stayed long enough to keep his friend alive.

9
My Grandma catches on

-Chewy-

They both looked down at Kent's pale face, his eyes still staring wide back at them.

"You ever seen a dead body before?" Chewy said, looking over to Clint's white face.

Clint shook his head without saying a word.

"Yeah, me neither." Chewy paused, staring back down at Kent and then said, "Are we supposed to call someone now or what?"

Clint shrugged to which Chewy lifted an eyebrow.

"You don't think we could just push him under the bed, you know, so that my mom doesn't see him, do you?"

Clint's wide, shocked eyes said it all.

"Yeah, that's what I thought too," Chewy said, dropping his vision back down to Kent's ghastly face.

Luckily for them, they didn't have to figure anything out. A second later, the front door slammed shut, and both boys turned around to look at Chewy's closed bedroom door. The only thought either of them could muster was that the soldier was back to finish the job, but an even greater fear fell upon them when they heard a voice they knew scream out.

"Hee-Chu!"

It was his mom's voice, and seeing Clint's buckled shoulders, Chewy knew he thought they were in trouble, but instead a sudden relief washed over Chewy. If it were his mom, she would have used his new name.

"We're in here!" Chewy screamed.

Clint tossed his head to Chewy with question marks in his eyes, and Chewy smiled. "Looks like finally, something's going our way. Now, we should be able to figure something out."

He reached out hitting the lever next to the door to pop it open from the outside. As soon as it swung past them, his mom marched in and glancing up at her eyes, Chewy saw the deep brown he knew to be his grandmother's. She didn't waste a second to start talking.

"We were looking for those stupid pins your mom wanted when it happened," she said, almost out of breath. "In that moment of weakness, I was able to take over. Your mom is one tough woman."

"You're not so easy yourself," Chewy said with a grin.

His grandmother's shoulders sank as if losing

much stress, and a small, sad smile stretched on her face.

"You aren't angry at me then?" she asked.

"I was the one who decided to do something stupid, like fight a ghost, not you."

His grandmother reached out and hugged him before Clint jumped in.

"I'm guessing by her not being crazy angry that this is your grandmother. In that case, I don't mean to butt in but…" he said, lowering his head to Kent in the middle of the room.

Chewy batted his eyes. He had somehow completely forgotten the dead body on his bedroom floor. He turned to his grandmother and explained everything.

Chewy had no idea what was going on in her head, hoping that it all made sense. The whole time he spoke, all his grandmother did was squint at the body with a finger to her lips. When he finished, she began nodding.

"So that's how he wants to play it," she remarked, withdrawing her finger.

"Who?" Chewy asked.

She shook her head.

"Never mind that for now," she said. "First, let me take stock of this place to make sure my hunch is correct."

Saying this, she charged out of the room only to pause briefly in front of the hall closet with a tilt of her head before moving into the rest of the house.

Clint leaned over to Chewy. "Is this good or bad?"

Chewy shrugged. "Let's find out."

Before even leaving the room, they both heard slamming noises in the kitchen and dashed outside. His grandmother was kicking around chairs, muttering to herself. Chewy looked to Clint before asking his grandmother what was going on.

"Your mother—ugh!" she screamed back.

"What?" Chewy said, tossing his head around the room as if his mom was in there hiding somewhere.

"Like you said, she blessed the doors to stop bridges from connecting with this house, but she only did all the standard doors. It never occurred to her that any door can become a bridge," she said, and pointed to the fridge door that was still hanging open, and then continued, "Not just that, but all of these cabinets are unblessed. If she had consulted with me, none of this would've happened in the first place."

His grandmother collapsed into a chair still muttering. Chewy tiptoed closer.

"So does that mean you have any idea what's going on?"

His grandmother nodded with a grim face before speaking.

"From your description of the attacker, I knew what it was instantly. Seeing the fridge door open only confirms it. We're dealing with a Jeoseung-Saja," she said and seeing no reaction on his face, added, "A Korean grim reaper."

Chewy made an "Oh!" expression, causing Clint to lean over asking what was up. Chewy whispered back, "Reapers." Clint froze in place.

Chewy kept watching his grandmother who was somewhat lost in her own thoughts as she continued.

"They're kind of like Yeomra's henchmen really. They go get the normal souls and make sure they arrive to the underground. They replaced his old workers because unlike them, sajas are impossible to bribe. Money is useless to them. Disgusting creatures."

Her face shriveled up as if eating a prune, and now Chewy understood why Gangnim had the same reaction thinking about them and their work. These creatures were ruthless, caring only about killing. There was no compassion—one thing Chewy had definitely felt in Gangnim.

"But when it comes to them and Gangnim," Chewy started, "besides their conduct, aren't both of them under Yeomra's control?"

His grandmother shook her head. "Sajas are mindless vultures that hang around car accidents and hospitals. They follow orders. On the other hand, Gangnim, although technically working for Yeomra, runs by his own rules. He doesn't take orders as long as he gets his job done."

Chewy was glad Clint didn't understand any of it. He was pretty sure Clint would have exploded.

"Then what can we do?" Chewy asked.

"In that regard, it looks like your mom did something right," she said, digging through her pockets until finally pulling out two dark pieces of metal.

"Is that them?" Chewy said, pushing Clint into a chair, so he didn't look so strange gawking at them.

"Yes, these will hide anything from Death's radar and thus hide you from sajas but sadly not Gangnim. They might just make what we have to do next a little easier," she said with a smile.

"Which is what?" Chewy said, taking a chair for himself as she passed the metal pins to him.

"Why—bring your friend back from the dead, of course!"

Chewy fluttered his eyes, looking at the hard metal that looked like strange hairpins in his hand. He had seen enough now to know this was no joke, and he smiled. Finally, his life was getting fun again.

10
I leave myself behind

-Chewy-

At the kitchen table, Chewy slipped the metal pins into his pocket as his grandmother jumped in, explaining everything.

"You remember the story of the door god your grandfather told you, yes?" she said with a snort.

Hearing her mention his grandfather, Chewy wondered if it was a good time to point out that he had been missing for a couple of weeks now. But seeing her reaction to his name, he pushed it aside, nodding to her question.

"Then you also remember how he became a god?" she paused, glancing at Clint before saying, "Make sure he knows what's going on too. He's going to come in handy."

A few images floated around in Chewy's head. He had met the door god not too long ago in person, recalling the old man's wispy beard and mischevious smile. His real name had been Nok-di-saeng. He was kind of Chewy's spiritual godfather.

Following his grandmother's advice, he answered her in English to keep Clint in the loop.

"Something about the door god," he started, turning back to his grandmother's strict face. "After his mom was killed he brought her back to life with some flowers. For doing so, he was rewarded by becoming a god."

She stared at him with upturned lips as if everything was clear now. He wrinkled his brow.

"Are you saying we're going to do the same for Kent?" he asked, noticing Clint's lowered eyebrows and worried glance.

"In the So-chon garden, there are various kinds of flowers. Each one possesses a different kind of effect. If we get the right one, we'll be able to fix this," she said, pausing with a worried look.

"What is it?" Chewy said, pushing her on.

She looked around the house as if trying to locate some hidden individual before looking back at them and then said, "The only thing is I don't know who is behind this. I have a feeling it's to lead you out of this house. Whoever it is knows you're safe here. By leaving, we're running a big risk."

"In what way?"

"Gangnim is a man of rules. If you break them, he becomes merciless. He expects you here on Wednesday, but by going after those flowers, you've officially broken your promise to him. I don't know what he will do to you then."

Chewy caught Clint's eye. He knew his friend was worried about exactly this kind of situation—one where he took on unnecessary danger, but he didn't know how to make Clint see that hiding a problem didn't fix anything. Due to his aquaphobia, Clint had grown accustomed to waiting for a solution to come along, for everything to just become good without addressing the bad. Chewy knew this didn't solve anything. In Korea, they did this all the time, hiding corruption and traditions that weakened them, all for what? To look good in the world's eyes? Chewy couldn't see the good in that.

He turned to his friend, ready for a conflict and detailed everything to him.

"I have to do this," he said afterwards. "There's no other way."

Clint's face had gone flat, and Chewy could tell he was angry.

"Did you not listen to anything I just told you back in the bedroom?"

Chewy turned back to his grandmother. He wasn't in the mood for another argument. This had to be done. Kent may have deserved a couple of broken bones, but he didn't deserve to be a part of Chewy's curse.

"Let's do this," he told her.

Immediately, she got up, closing the fridge door. She darted off to the bedroom and came back with some candles, essences, and her traditional clothes. As she slipped them over her own pair, she explained.

"To get there I'm going to have to open up a blind bridge to the gods' realms. Now, you must remember while there, time goes faster than it does here. Your journey may take months, but by the time you return, it may've only been a day or two here, so don't worry. The reverse is true if you go to the underground. Time seems to work in layers that way."

She lit a wick of incense and then continued.

"After you leave, I'm going to cleanse the house to make sure no spirits can enter without our explicit permission given to them first. This should protect the house and the portal you leave from, but unfortunately, while you're gone, you will be in the open, so be careful, my little Hee-Chu."

Chewy hugged his grandmother and then turned to Clint's downturned face. As his grandmother began the ritual for the door bridge, Chewy pulled Clint aside.

"Look," he whispered, "this is not what I planned for, either. But it has to be done."

"Running off alone?" Clint snorted.

"I know it won't help anything. Me reviving Kent is only tending to a symptom. In order to fix it all, we need to know what we're dealing with. For that, we need my grandfather."

"Then what are you saying?"

Before responding, Chewy reached out holding on to the sleeve of Clint's jacket. As he did so, he dropped one of the metal pins into a pocket. Even though things might be dangerous, he wanted to make sure his best friend was protected.

"While I'm gone, I need you and Su Bin to find him. But I want you to know I am afraid because all of this means something much worse is going to happen. I'm not taking things lightly."

Clint's face changed completely, his eyes trembling.

"What do you mean worse?"

"Like you said, Kent's power is linked to mine, which means whatever happens to me, something only slightly worse happens to him. The opposite is true, too."

Clint's eyes grew with realization before he spoke.

"So if he's dead…" he trailed off.

Chewy picked it up, nodding. "Exactly, then whatever is one step worse than death is waiting for me."

With that, he turned to the newly blessed refrigerator and took a quick glance at both his grandmother and Clint before stepping into the door bridge, leaving the Earth behind.

11
How My Grandfather Joined The War

-Joong Bum-

It all started with the war.

And only now that I think of it, does it seem strange. Nowadays, most Korean boys want to avoid their army duties as much as possible. But for me, I couldn't wait. Han Joong had already left, and the only thing I heard around the house and the neighborhood was how amazing and brave he was. I can still remember how Sae-rim's eyes glowed at every mention of his name.

So I joined the army—and really, none too soon. The Americans had already jumped into the war, and the North had all but pushed their way down to the southern tip.

My house was lucky. We were out in the country enough to go overlooked by the soldiers of either side. In this way, I could've avoided the war entirely. Though we knew any day a troop could march by taking me with it. My mother just hoped it wasn't a Northern one.

And of course, the small town nearby had their problems, particularly the scrimmage that ended with Sae-rim's house blowing up—the one that killed her parents. But this isn't about Sae-rim.

Within days of enlisting, I was trained and pushed along with the UN forces, battle by battle, getting our country's land back. Fighting side by side, I made a few friends—something hard to do in the countryside. Among them was Jeong. That was his family name, but everyone just called him that.

What a round little man he was! Well, he was a boy, I guess, as we all were. But he didn't look like a soldier, which could have been said for me as well. While Jeong was quite big, I was skin and bones. Maybe because of this, we grew close. Outsiders stick together.

I remember one sunny day. We were marching north, listening to the gunfire in the distance. It was miles off, which meant we wouldn't see any action for a good day or two if we were lucky. That's when Jeong started jumping up and down.

"What is it?" I asked him.

"I know this place," he said, pointing to a set of large mountains. "Just beyond that ridge is my hometown."

A large smile painted itself across his face. With all his fat, this just made him look jollier.

"It's almost sundown," I said, jabbing him with my elbow. "I'm sure if you ask…"

He was already thinking the same thing and ran

ahead to catch up with the captain. His short legs spit up dust behind him.

And we were right. That night, after crossing the ridge, we stayed in Jeong's hometown. Most towns we went through were very gracious and helpful to us soldiers. Many times, with our coming, the enemy had just retreated, and the rumors were the North wasn't very kind.

They tended to demand much from the towns they traveled through, taking food and living in the homes as they wished. Most people allowed it. They were afraid of what the consequences might be, but that didn't mean they tried their best to help, unlike they did for us.

We were welcomed thoroughly along with our American allies. And they took us into their homes with warm hearts. They gave us blankets to sleep on their floors and fed us with what little food they had, which was also what little food they had kept hidden from the Northern soldiers. We were in this together. You could feel it.

But that night, Jeong and I got the royal treatment. His mother had one of her chickens killed and cooked for us, and we ate as much as we could, all the while she told stories to me about him as a kid.

"You know he used to climb our fence at night to go looking for boar. He thought he was a hunter," she snorted, poking Jeong's belly. "If anything, with that pudge, I was bound to hear a real hunter had shot my boy, mistaking him for a boar."

Despite these words, Jeong's mother pushed more food in front of her son. And you could clearly see the family resemblance. She was on the hefty side as well. Whenever not talking about her son, she'd look me up and down with worry.

"Son," she said, "don't you have food where you come from?"

I laughed. No matter how much I ate, I never gained a pound. The same was true for Han Joong but at least he had muscle to hide his thinness. By the end of my stay in the army, I'd have quite a bit of muscle too.

Near the end of the night, his mother pulled me aside into the dirt-scarred backyard while she sank her beefy hands into a large bucket of dirty dishes. Jeong was already dozing on the floor in the living room.

"You seem like a good, young man," she said, lifting her ball of curly, gray hair so as to squint at me as if looking into my soul.

I thanked her for the compliment, bowing slightly.

"Then I have a request for you," she said and stopped. Tears were already sprouting in her eyes, but she looked down to keep them hidden from me. I wanted to say something but felt it would be rude to interrupt. Finally, her voice returned.

"My boy…he is healthy. There's no doubt about that," she said, smiling for a second to lighten the mood before her voice deepened with seriousness. "But I can't fool myself. He's a weakling—inside. He doesn't have the heart to be a soldier, or at least the kind of soldier that will make it through this war."

I tried to open my mouth to disagree with her, but she thrust a soapy finger in my face to hush me up.

"A mother knows these things. There are dangers out there—waiting for him—that if they find him," she shook her head, "he won't make it through…unless he has help."

She lowered her eyebrows on the word "help," and I knew what she meant. I was supposed to be that help. What these dangers were, I had no idea, but I didn't even think about asking. And then, at last, it was my time to speak.

"Don't worry, Mrs. Soon, I will bring your son back to you. As long as we're together, nothing will happen to him."

I cannot describe to you the feeling that came to me then, seeing the joy in her eyes. I believe the way she looked at me is the way most people would react to seeing an angel. I have never had such a feeling again in my entire life.

I slept well that night. It was impossible not to. I felt so at home and safe, not since the day I left my country home had I felt that warm.

The next morning, we were called bright and early to join ranks. After heads were counted, we began our march to leave, but before we reached the town's limits, Jeong's mother came running.

She screamed after him and catching us, tossed her arms around me, and then him for one last hug. As she embraced her son, she slipped a necklace around his thick neck. I did my best to hide my shock that it could fit at all.

"This was from your father," she said to him, and the way her voice lowered I knew something had happened recently that brought about his absence. She wanted to keep it hushed to hide the sadness. "He gave it to me the first time we met. He would be proud of you."

He smiled with tears in his eyes, hugged his mother one last time, and then we were off. He mentioned none of what happened to his father, despite all the family stories I shared with him. I didn't press either. I figured we were all allowed some secret grief. I knew I had mine.

Thinking about all of this now, I see how silly life is. Had we known what was in store for us, maybe Jeong and I would've hidden out in his mother's home. Our lives could've been different. But that's not how things were meant to go.

And so, a week later our troop was overrun.

Part II: Upper Realms

12
Old Gangnim catches on as well

-Gangnim-

As soon as Chewy stepped through the door bridge to the upper realms, a ripple went through the spiritual world, and Gangnim, leaning backward in his chair, caught a disturbance in the gaekgwis—the wandering spirits that surrounded the underground. Something wasn't right with them, and he knew their sensitivity was for a reason. However, something else entirely was on his mind and he looked back to the table, careful of the tea in front of him.

After getting the job as messenger, Gangnim took over the small cottage he had first met Yeomra in. It kept him grounded, remembering what he had lost up above. Yeomra offered him many other places, but he preferred something simple, keeping even the table as his desk, which he sat at now, perusing files for what bothered him.

As he compared quite a few of the papers, there appeared to be overlapping reports, notations that seemed inconsistent and at other times impossible.

Tracing them back, it all seemed to have started roughly a month ago. The why of the situation still eluded him, and he was pondering over this very issue when a dark figure stepped from the shadows in the corner.

He didn't look up or act surprised at this. He was used to Yeomra entering in this way and spoke to him immediately.

"You know he's going for the resurrection flower?"

Yeomra snorted, slipping into the nearest chair.

"That old mu-dang knows how to play." Then he reached out, lifting Gangnim's tea to his nose for a whiff and continued, "Lemon—good choice!"

"My question is," Gangnim said, dismissing the dark god's words, "why would he go after them in the first place?"

Yeomra gave him an innocent I-don't-know face before drawing in a large slurp of tea. Gangnim sighed heavily. He was used to this subterfuge—over a million years' worth. These games were getting old.

"I could always make you a cup," he offered.

Yeomra waved exaggeratedly. "You don't plan to stay long anyway." He coughed to change subjects. "Which brings up an issue of my own. While you're diddling around in the upper realms, you might as well take care of something for me."

Gangnim brought his eyes back up, glaring at him as if to say, "What?"

Yeomra peered over the teacup at him with steam in his face.

"The garden," he mouthed.

Gangnim shook his head. "You can't do this yourself?"

Yeomra set the cup down and lifted a finger of rebuttal. "Oh, I would. However, my sajas can't go to the upper realms, and it's sort of looked down upon when gods do those types of things."

Gangnim bowed his head and, taking on a mocking tone, said, "Is that all?"

Yeomra squinted at him, kicking his feet up onto the table.

"You've had this job for too long," he snarled. "I liked you better when you were open with your disdain for me. You used to love throwing it in my face. Now all I get is this saracasm."

"Even I can change," Gangnim said with a shrug and stuck his lips out in innocence, causing the death god to purse his in distrust.

"Looking over past reports, I found some kind of anomaly," Gangnim continued, pointing at the files before him. "You wouldn't know anything about that, would you?"

Yeomra lifted an eyebrow, blowing steam away from the cup.

"It seems our radar has been picking up…something unusual. This can't be a mistake," Gangnim continued, keeping his eye on the papers before him.

"That old witch," the dark god muttered. "She's

full of tricks. I'll send some scouts to flush out what she's up to."

Gangnim flicked his wrist at it as if to say, "Whatever you think is best."

"They're on their way now," Yeomra said, giving a snap of finality, and then continued, "This upsets you?"

He wasn't upset. He was overjoyed. Gangnim knew Yeomra had just tipped his hand. This was one trick the death god was not responsible for, and Gangnim's brain reeled trying to piece it together. But, above all, he had to act normal if he wished to keep this advantage.

"Why should it?" he said. "I know where my mark is. He's broken away from his safe house on the way to So-chon. He's in the open."

Gangnim pushed the papers back into the file and patted them against the table to tidy them up before finally looking at Yeomra once again. There was still one more thing he had to do if he wanted to keep Yeomra in the dark. Thinking of it, he found it hard not to smile.

"I'll see him, shortly," he resumed. "Just figured I'd run it by you first."

Yeomra bloated out his cheeks in faux surprise. "By all means don't let me hold you up."

Gangnim grabbed the large armor hanging on another chair and slipped it over his head before taking his sword. He bowed to the still reclining Yeomra and went for the door, stopping behind his chair.

"One last thing," he said, catching Yeomra's twisted neck. "When I gave Chewy the courtesy call for his upcoming death, he mentioned a ghost had given him that scar. Said he was ordered more or less."

"Are you implying—"

Before Yeomra could finish, Gangnim plunged his sword into the back of the chair through the dark lord's chest. The dark figure slumped forward, and finding himself pinned to the chair, coughed before he spoke up again.

"I hate it when you do that," he seethed, his hand grabbing around the clean blade.

"I hate it when you meddle in my special cases," Gangnim muttered. He knew neither he nor Yeomra could be killed. At best, they could be detained. He hadn't done this in years, and he continued, "If you wanted any one of them, all you had to do was ask."

"That's what this is about?" Yeomra spat out, nodding toward the sword.

Gangnim raised an eyebrow to say, "Yes."

Yeomra rolled his eyes. "I merely had one of my sajas go and kill his crippled friend. I left your precious special case alone."

Gangnim stuck out his jaw as if pondering something of great importance and then picked up his helmet from behind the door before turning back to the dark god. "If that's true, what are you going to do about her?"

"Her?" the dark god said, twisting his head to

Gangnim by the door. A pinch of discomfort from the sword washed over his face.

"The grandmother. She's blessed the house and as far as the gaekgwi are reacting, it looks like she's in possession of some silver pins. Your sajas are going to have a hard time now with any other non-special cases you have in mind."

"What do you care?" Yeomra said, peeking back down at the sword.

"I don't. And as long as you leave Chewy to me, you won't find yourself stuck to anymore chairs. Whatever else you have planned is your business."

Gangnim finally smiled and placed the helmet on his head, covering his face in shadows.

"Don't worry about it," Yeomra said, placing his hands up. "That old woman has only so many tricks up her sleeve. One day, she'll run out. Before that happens, I'll just have to apply a little pressure. Luckily, I have just the person for the job."

Gangnim opened the door to leave, but hearing a faint cough from behind, he turned back around.

"Aren't you forgetting something?" the dark god asked, looking down at the blade again.

"You're right," Gangnim said, and reached behind the door for another sword. "I may need one after all."

Yeomra lowered his eyelids in disdain. "I take it back. I've never liked you."

And at that, Gangnim stepped out, leaving the

dark god to figure his own way off the sword that held him.

13
My Grandma straightens everything out

-Chewy's Grandmother-

The mu-dang grabbed the candles from the top shelf in her closet, careful not to close its door fully. Even a mundane task like this was welcomed after her three weeks of exile. As much as she hated being shut away from her family—a family she had only recently reconnected with—the time alone was needed and good for her in a way.

She took the candles into the living room, taking stock of the perimeter. The ritual needed open space and as she aligned the candles along the cardinal lines, a shudder ran through her. She recalled the lost feeling she experienced with the old protection being pierced by one of Yeomra's sajas.

Her daughter was at the local hardware store. She had just picked up a set of silver pins in the back when the alarm rippled through her. She dropped to the ground, weakened, believing it was too late. They had her son. In that instant, the mu-dang took over, knowing this may be her only chance.

With candles lit, she pushed the coffee table and this vision aside. The mid-March sky was darkening and she wanted to get this done before nightfall. The hiss of her tea drew her attention to the kitchen, specifically the refrigerator, and an image of Chewy walking through it an hour earlier surfaced in her head. That boy definitely had his grandfather's blood, all right.

He had lied to her every chance he could, using that trick his grandfather taught him in order to keep her out of his head. Did he think she wouldn't find out? She had felt it instantly when he connected Korea and America with a door bridge. She was not so foolish, but she realized, in time, it would come in handy. That wasn't what bothered her.

She pulled the teapot off the stove and poured a cup for herself at the kitchen table. By the time she finished her ritual, it would be the perfect temp, and she returned to the living room, feeling the energy build around her. When the moment was right, she began to sway and chant.

The thing that did bother her was the memory that haunted her time while she was locked away. She reviewed it frequently, knowing there was something hidden in it, and the time apart allowed her to sniff it out.

Roughly a month earlier, Chewy got stitches for the scar beneath his nose. Afterwards, he led all of them upstairs to check on his comatose friends. As expected, they had fully recovered. The halls were alive with nurses jumping from room to room and the general sigh of relief that all the parents had. Chewy led them to Becky's room.

From inside her daughter's head, the mu-dang could see her grandson had a special bond with this girl, but soon she came face to face with the strange mystery that followed her every waking thought.

When they entered Becky's room, her parents beamed with arms around their daughter, talking to a flustered doctor and, upon seeing Chewy, smiled more greatly.

They were surprised to see him and pushed the curtain aside to welcome everyone in. There had been a miracle after all, and soon Chewy's mom found herself talking to these over joyous parents, using Su Bin as an interpreter for her words. Not knowing any of Chewy's tricks, their thoughts rang loud and clear. For her, an interpreter was useless.

"He's been here non-stop. He's really kept our spirits up with all his visits," they said.

The mu-dang cringed. These were distressed parents and even the images they brought up in their heads went unchecked, but she saw them, and in that moment, saw Chewy's as well.

For him, he had only visited once with his cousin, Su Bin. What these parents expressed was wrong except their thoughts proved they weren't lying. Some version of Chewy had visited them—that was true—but the picture of Chewy in their heads had something the real Chewy didn't have until late: a faint, white scar beneath his nose. This was impossible because Chewy had gained that scar only a matter of minutes ago. What they spoke of spanned weeks into the past.

Her body began to slow down, feeling the room tighten with force and she stopped, certain that this would hold Death and his legion out for now. The only way in was if they were invited, and nobody would be that foolish, but in that way, she had to be careful. Death knew how to make fools of people.

She grabbed the nearest chair for balance. The ritual had exhausted her, and she made her way slowly into the kitchen and took a seat at the table. She was right. The tea was now the perfect temp, and she lifted it to her nose. What a bitter smell! It would be good, and a smile came to her face.

In order to save Chewy, she needed a plan. And what this old memory meant was that her plan had already worked. She had proof. The hard part now was figuring out what the plan was in the first place. She wished she had left a note for herself. Thinking this, she stopped. Maybe, she had something even better.

But old Yeomra had something planned too, and she was willing to let him enjoy it. When it came to gods, they owned the playing field of time. She wasn't going to pretend to have an upper hand, but in the end, if she focused and played things right, she might be able to not only get Chewy out of his claws but deal out a little payback as well. In that respect, maybe she and Chewy were a little bit the same.

And she sat enjoying her tea while devising her plan, knowing the next step fully depended on what flowers Chewy brought back with him. If not, she might have to go on a little trip herself.

14
My Good Friend: Sam-jok-o

-Chewy-

As soon as Chewy stepped through the door, his head swirled much like the first time, and he forgot his reason for coming. In that way, his grandmother was right. Time was different depending on which level he was on.

The first couple of hours he spent wandering a path in a daze as he collected himself. He wasn't sure how he didn't recall it the last time he was here, or maybe he had fallen out of the door god's favor. Either way, he felt lost.

Soon he found himself in a thick wood that through branches, he was able to spot far off mountains that never seemed to get any closer. The sky was dull and the earth smelled wet, which made everything all the more eerie.

His first night was spent curled up next to what looked like an oak tree; however, the darkness made it hard to see, and he stayed bundled on the piled leaves not feeling cold at all.

By morning, the sky was palely lit again, and he continued forward, only believing that if he kept going in one direction, eventually something would appear. And, eventually something did. It only took a full month of endless walking.

He traipsed into a clearing and enjoyed the sun on his face and shoulders after having been in that forest for so long. Then he smiled. There in front of him were the bare tree from his visit before and the seventy-seven paths stretching out into the mountains beyond. The only thing missing was the door god, and a dread sank into him. He felt that maybe with Death on his trail, the silly, old man had abandoned him.

Before this thought grew any further in his head, a voice cracked down to him as if cackling.

"He's a little bit busy, you know."

Chewy darted his head around but found no one. Was this another of the door god's tricks? The last time, he had taken Chewy's rice cake.

"You needn't worry about his tricks. He always has much greater plans in store, unlike his friend."

This time the voice had spoken long enough for Chewy to find its source, which seemed to be hidden in the tree above him. He only saw a deep shadow.

"How do you know these things?" Chewy asked, hoping to determine if his hunch was right. Staring deadpan at the darkness, he saw it move.

"I'm no harm whatsoever," it said, skipping down the branches. "Most people don't even notice me anymore, or just shoo me away."

As it hopped from branch to branch, the sunlight lit up its shape, and Chewy saw it was a large, black bird. *They have strange animals here*, he thought until it dropped down onto the bottom branch, and he froze. It had three legs.

"That's what most people do—that is when they really pay attention," it said and then cawed as if laughing.

"You're a Sam-jok-o," Chewy stumbled over his words. He had read stories about it in some mythological comic books as a kid. That explained the nice day. It was rumored to be the bearer of the sun.

"I'm the bearer of many things," it mumbled, clearly having read Chewy's mind. "I also guide the lost, depending on who you ask."

It made its final leap and landed on the rock at the foot of the tree, bouncing its head up and down as if tasting the air. Chewy took a seat on another rock nearby. A rest was needed, and besides, the bird may have answers.

"I have more than that," it said, tilting its head to wink at him, and Chewy couldn't help thinking that all mythical creatures were a little bit mischievous. Then Chewy's eyes grew big, and he put up his hands.

"Not that it's bad," he said, knowing full well the bird had read his mind, and tried to explain, "I'm quite mischievous myself. I guess we're the same that way."

"You are right there," it cawed. "We all come from the same pool, but we definitely aren't the same. You, for instance, have a long road ahead of you."

Chewy lowered his head. He wasn't looking forward to more walking.

"Oh no, not that," the bird corrected, twitching its head. "You're getting closer to where you physically need to go, but your other path is much longer."

Chewy lifted his head and an eyebrow. What was this bird talking about?

"It is always hard to see the design of things in the beginning," the bird croaked again. "It is because you are a part of it. Eventually, after everything is done, the picture will become clear."

Chewy wrinkled his nose up at the bird. "Do all mythical beings have to talk in riddles?"

The bird looked bug-eyed at him before answering. "Only the good ones do."

Chewy wasn't positive, but it looked like the bird smirked at him.

"I don't mean to be rude," Chewy started again, "but you have any idea which one I'm supposed to take?"

The bird popped off the rock onto the dirt path and shifted its beak over each avenue. He stopped at one that looked like two paths crisscrossing each other.

"Not yet time for this one, eh?" it said.

Chewy looked at the two interwoven dirt lines,

foggily remembering something about them, but dismissed it with a shake of his head.

"You know or not?"

The bird glared back at him, a glint in its black eyes.

"Don't get testy with me. Deep inside, you just reacted to those two roads. You're afraid and you should be." It paused and then pointed with its beak to a path on the other side, near the tree. "That's the one you want for now."

Chewy started off toward it, wondering what this bird was going on about. He didn't feel anything, especially fear.

"It's natural to be afraid. We all have our faults—even a special case, like you," it cawed after him.

Chewy froze again. *A special case?* He whirled back around toward the bird. Yet another person was calling him special, and he had no idea why. When Gangnim did it, it was out of duty and job. This sounded more like what that old ghost had said.

"What do you know?" he asked, watching the bird in the distance hop forward a bit.

"I know opinions don't seem to be so much your problem," it said, tilting its head to acknowledge such difficulty. "But something much bigger is coming your way. We're all quite interested to see how you'll do."

Chewy suddenly felt like a much larger audience was watching him, and he carefully shifted his head around. But, there was nothing but the bird.

"Sometimes the very thing that makes us great is the same thing that causes our downfall," it started up again, extending its neck.

Chewy shook his head again. This bird was just wasting his time. And he resumed his march toward the mountains. Before he got too far, the bird cawed one last thing to him.

"You better walk faster than that," it said, lowering its voice as it spoke to itself. "You have more than one shadow to deal with."

A short time later, Chewy's figure was but a dot on the horizon. The bird had watched him the whole time and was about to hop back to its perch when a shadow caught it by surprise. Looking up, it saw a darkened face and a body covered in armor. It recognized Gangnim instantly.

"Hoping to be gone before you came," it mumbled, jittering away from Gangnim's large form.

"So the boy was here?" he asked.

The bird stopped and eyed him with distrust. "I don't have to tell you that."

Gangnim smiled. "You just did."

The bird fluttered its wings in anger, retaking its seat on the rock beside the tree.

"You best leave things alone," it warned him.

He lowered down, placing his elbows on his knees to get a better look at the creature. "What have you overheard, old bird? I know you watch them at their games."

It snorted. "Their game is much bigger than you think."

Gangnim righted himself. He fully knew this creature would give him nothing but riddles, and he looked off into the distant. Chewy's silhouette was gone, but he knew the way. The scar seemed to be beckoning him forward, and he withdrew his sword.

15
My Cousin's Problem

-Su Bin-

Su Bin heard the door shut instantly and sat up, fluttering her eyes to adjust to the darkness. It wasn't too hard to see with the sun creeping in through the window. She checked the clock. Six-thirty.

"Who's there?" she said in Korean, looking to the shadowy corner where her closet lay hidden. Slowly, Clint stepped into the light, and she smiled. He looked embarrassed for seeing her this way, and she looked down at her pajamas. Weren't they the same pair she had worn in America?

"I thought maybe it was Chewy," she said, switching over to English as she pulled the covers back. She smirked at him turning away as to not watch her get out of bed. *What a silly boy!*

With his back turned, Clint mumbled to her. "That's why I'm here."

Su Bin froze. Since Chewy had told her about

Gangnim's visit, she had spent each moment worrying over what would happen next. Every evening, nightmares of hearing her mother getting the news of her cousin's death haunted her. Believing now that it had come true, she hoped it was painless.

Clearly, she sat silent in thought for too long because Clint turned to look at her.

"No, no," he said, putting up his hands at the sight of her moist eyes. "It's not that—well, not exactly."

He extended a hand to ask whether he could sit down, and she waved him over, patting the bed sheet next to her. He took the bed's far corner instead.

"First of all, Chewy is alright for now," Clint started, and Su Bin lowered her shoulders hearing this as he continued, "But I can't say as much for Kent."

Su Bin lifted her eyebrows. A lot had happened and she sat quietly, watching his lips intently as he described everything from the past day. By the end, she couldn't believe any of it. In a way, she felt Kent got what he deserved and marveled even more at Chewy's ability to forgive enough to try bringing this monster boy back from the dead.

"He's quite amazing, isn't he?" she said, referring to her cousin.

Clint shrugged. "I guess."

She wrinkled her brow at this half-hearted answer, recalling how both had acted toward each other the previous Saturday. Something was definitely going on between them—particularly Clint. It was all the more strange because last month he couldn't stop raving about his best friend. Now, everything had changed, and it made her curious why.

"You two okay?" she questioned.

"Never better," Clint said, smiling, and Su Bin squinted at him. She had heard enough from Chewy that it didn't take special powers to tell when Clint was lying. She decided not to push any further at the moment. There were more important topics to discuss and besides, she'd get it out of him eventually. And she grinned, thinking of how much fun it would be.

Clint wrinkled his brow at her before starting up again. "Anyways, before he left, he wanted me to do a couple of things…with you."

She perked up, her eyes still in little slits. She found his embarrassment for his feelings toward her particularly endearing, and she would've felt the same…if anyone else were around. But she was happy to finally have time with just him. She wouldn't have to hide anything.

"What exactly do we have to do?" she squeaked.

"Well, for one, his grandfather," he said, pausing at the reaction on her face.

She didn't know how to tell him and felt like a failure already.

"I've tried six times since Saturday," she said,

lowering her head. "Still nothing."

Clint nodded glumly. "He expected as much. So he wants us to go check on him. I have the password for his front door."

Su Bin's head sprang up again. Maybe things were going to work out. She really hoped she could fix Chewy's problems. She still felt a little guilty about him getting the scar below his nose, after all, if she had checked the room better, the ghost would've never been able to hunt Chewy down in the first place.

"On top of that," Clint added, raising a finger to grab her attention again, "he wants us to set up a door bridge from his house—to make checking up on his grandfather a little bit easier."

"Good idea," she said and jumped off the bed, grabbing a black and white checkered dress from off her desk chair. Clint lowered his head and looked at the wall. Su Bin smiled at this. Did he really think she'd be crazy enough to change in front of him? She understood more and more why Chewy had him as a best friend. He was quite ridiculous.

"For now, I've got to get ready for school. Stop back again late tonight, and we'll see what we can do," she said with a smile.

He nodded, smirking back at her uncomfortably, and headed toward the closet. It looked like he had something else to say, but he just turned and left.

That night, Su Bin got home a little past ten thirty. Her mom was busy preparing a late dinner as Su Bin usually munched on kim-bap between lessons. At the same time, she had figured out what to do when Clint came over the bridge again. They would need to do this in the early hours—it was the only way to keep her parents clueless to not only her leaving, but there being a boy in her room as well. Shutting the front door quietly behind her, she entered the kitchen with half-shut eyes.

"Math class okay?" her mother intoned in Korean. Su Bin answered back with a weak "yes" and took a seat as her mom whisked over a bowl of rice with an egg on top and another bowl of kimchi soup next to it.

Su Bin wasted no time devouring it and not just out of hunger. It was cold outside and, unlike America, the lobbies and halls in most buildings were unheated, being nothing more than protection from the wind. Getting some hot soup in her, she began to feel her body thaw.

But as she ate, this thought led her into others about America. She missed it for so many more reasons than warm hallways.

While there, she had finally gotten close to Chewy and was afraid that upon his return to Korea—where good scores mattered more than anything—a different division might resurface between them, namely her mom. She looked up at her mom traipsing around the kitchen while her father watched TV in the bedroom.

Su Bin hoped that if she spent a little more time with Chewy, they'd have something together that was much stronger, that she'd have someone permanently in her corner. With no siblings, he was the only other family member even close to the same age as her. Korean families were shrinking.

Another thing she missed were her friends. True, she didn't have many. Her main friend was Susie, and Su Bin felt in the beginning that Susie had only befriended her to get back at Chewy. But they had a lot in common. Susie was a perfectionist and, above all, she knew boys—something Su Bin thought of a lot, but knew very little about.

She knew she wasn't good-looking—by Korean standards, at least—and Susie was able to help her see how girls got attention from boys, especially American boys.

In Korea, cute was always high in demand. Su Bin saw it in every K-pop group or singer she watched. The girls were sugary sweet and comically positive.

But America! Su Bin shook her head thinking about it as she ate her rice. Being strong wasn't necessarily a bad thing there…and she was a little too much like Chewy. She wanted to be strong. She wanted to speak out, only because she thought she never would.

And she looked up at her mom who, bent over

the stove, was mixing and stirring, getting another platter ready for her father.

Su Bin didn't want this kind of life—not that it was bad—but she wanted to make her own, and this brought her back to her parents. In that way, she was jealous of Chewy. Chewy's parents were much more open to new ideas, but not hers, especially her mom. She was far too conservative to ever let Su Bin pick her own future, no less her own boy, and her thoughts briefly returned to Clint. And she smiled.

She just hoped, one day, she'd find enough strength to speak her mind. In that way, she wished even Susie were still an influence in her life. Susie was always unrelenting.

16
Even Susie can connect some dots

-Susie-

The minefield of mud and slush deterred Susie little on the way to school. In fact, she barely noticed it at all, her mind drifting in and out as a cool March wind blew over her.

Her brain kept returning to a dream of hers—a dream all the more weird because she had had it now for two nights in a row. She felt she was missing something.

It always started out the same with a normal enough trip to the nearby mall. She could see the avenues of cars in the parking lot, and the beating sun glinting off their windshields, but it was upon entering the mall that the world grew eerie. Most of the stores had their metal linked gates drawn down, and despite the parked cars, barely a person was in sight. And that's when it would always happen. A sense of loss would sink over her as she suddenly saw a dark creature with a large black hat slip along the shadows and benches as if zoning in on her personally.

For some reason, at this moment, Becky always popped up next to her, whispering something while pointing at the shadowy figure. What was she telling her? Susie squinted as she skipped over a particularly large puddle. The words always avoided her, and she returned to the dream.

The dark creature then moved closer to them, extending a long arm, and it would touch Becky, sending her to the floor as if she were a marionette with its strings cut. Instantly, her limp body was enveloped in a hospital bed as the storefronts morphed into hospital walls. At this point, Susie's dream always ended with her waking up in a sweat.

She shook her head, her blond hair flipping behind her in a spring gust. Dreams! Don't they just take the events of our everyday lives and mix them all together? Still, something sat uneasily in her as she dissected it again.

The mall made sense. She was there as often as possible. For it to be the background of a dream was nothing unusual. But Becky being in it, well, that might have some more important meaning.

She looked around her, catching the gap in the fence to school up ahead. She thought for a second Becky might be around her somewhere—one of those weird coincidences where you think of someone and then they appear, but she saw no one, hearing the screams of children playing up ahead.

Becky was in the hospital for over two weeks recently. She was the third student from Grover Elementary to be hospitalized with some mysterious coma. And then, roughly three weeks ago, it all just ended with them waking up as healthy as they were before. No doctor could explain it. All the symptoms just disappeared.

Was that why Becky was in her dream? Susie only visited her once in the hospital, and it was more because her mom made her. She and Becky had been growing apart for a while now. Not to mention Becky's fascination with Chewy. That was a truly divisive issue between them. Becky was just beginning to turn around when Chewy came along and messed everything up.

Susie snapped her eyes wide open. *Chewy!*

Instead of the dream, an old memory shimmered into view as she stared at the sparkling sidewalk of puddles. When she had visited Becky, she saw Chewy sneak out as if not wanting to be noticed. It didn't register before, but now, it seemed strange, mainly because, as she focused on the memory more, it seemed he looked different, but what was it?

She clenched her eyes shut, drawing up the image, and slowly, the lines drew sharper, and she saw it, there beneath his nose. It was something that hadn't been there before. Did this all have something to do with Chewy?

She entered through the fence, taking the side blacktop to maneuver around the muddy field where a makeshift game of football was taking place. Generally, she stopped to watch, to pinpoint Blair—a boy she had only recently realized was stylish in her own manner—but the thought of Chewy had firmly attached itself to her brain, and she mindlessly continued over to the older kid's side of the school. Along the way, she saw Tom and would've passed him by as well, except he looked unusual, not just because of his saddened face, but because he was utterly alone.

"Where's Kent?" she asked, stopping next to him with a toss of her head for emphasis as to Kent's whereabouts.

The large boy shrugged, his cheeks jiggling.

She scanned his face. Something was wrong.

"What?" she said. Normally, she wouldn't have even inquired, but as of recent, she and Kent had a common bond: hating Chewy Noh. She had even been the one to tip Kent off over a month ago to Chewy's plans on stealing a test. It must've been good information because Kent was happy for weeks afterwards.

The large boy shook his head.

"I don't know," he said.

Susie grabbed the bridge of her nose. She rarely spoke to him and now realized why. His communication skills were greatly lacking.

"Why don't you know why?"

His eyes grew large and wet. "He's missing."

"Missing," she said, straightening her back. "Since when?"

"Two days ago."

She went bug-eyed. The same time her strange dream had started. She lowered an eyebrow at her silliness. It was just coincidence. Nothing more.

"I know he's done it before," Tom started again. "Running away and stuff. I mean, he always came back, but this time I don't think that's what's going on."

She put her arms on her waist, trying to look concerned. "Why would you say that?"

Tom scrunched up his face, a cheek bulging under one squashed eye.

"I think it has something to do with what happened last fall," he said, lowering his voice. "With the fire."

Chewy's fire? She nodded for him to continue. Tom knew she and Kent were close so it was okay to speak.

"Before the fire started, he and Chewy were saying something—something about his mom and a secret. It didn't make much sense to me, but afterwards, Kent was all strange."

Susie wrinkled her brow.

"His mom?" she said absent-mindedly. She had no idea how she could've overlooked it.

Chewy's mom was sick early last fall. And as she connected the dots, other things seemed to appear. Come winter, three students including Becky fell sick. And now Kent was missing. She was beginning to see a trend and noticed that Tom was still talking.

"I tried to get it out of Chewy, but he just acted like he didn't know what it was about, and anyways, he seems to be gone now too."

And now Chewy was gone too echoed in Susie's head. *That was it!* Something was going on here, and the only factor linking all of it together seemed to be Chewy.

"Tell me if anything else pops up," she mumbled, stumbling away from him, half-dazed.

Things had changed fast, and for the rest of the day not another thought rose in her head besides what might be going on with Chewy. And she knew in order to find out, the first thing she'd have to do is check out that house of his.

17
The So-chon Flower Garden

-Chewy-

The path Chewy took led him back into a woods, twisting and turning until he believed he would never find the place, and it was at that moment that he saw an open, rusted-over gate covered in vines.

He peeked in, and the sight overwhelmed him. There were rows upon rows of different shaped and colored flowers, trailing off to the horizon. Among this rainbow, little girls in pink dresses trotted along, watering each bud. Their long, black hair was tied around their heads, covering their ears. Scattered throughout the garden were small, stone structures like ruins from old palaces with domed tops and peaceful shade beneath. He had never seen anything like it.

He stepped in with caution, fully believing retrieving the resurrection flower from them would be a great task and was ready for battle when a thin, young man stepped out of one of the building's shadows. He did not look like any kind of warrior and came up with his arms wide.

"Welcome to the So-chon Flower Garden," he said, smiling. "My name is Halla-kkungi. I'm the flower warden here. Please come, sit down. You must be tired."

Chewy scratched his head at this puffy haired man but eventually nodded in agreement. A bit of rest did sound good. He couldn't recall ever walking so much before in his whole life, and only now, as he recounted his journey, did he realize it had taken him over six months. He hoped what his grandmother said was right; otherwise, upon returning, he would see a completely different world. Then again, maybe that would be interesting, he thought with a smirk.

Chewy followed the loose-robed man to a stone bench in the shade and relaxed as the man clapped his hands for one of the young flower girls to fetch them water.

"I'm sorry to say," he restarted, "we only have water to offer. This is a garden after all."

Chewy waved it away with a don't-worry-about-it look on his face. Halla-kkungi had yet to stop smiling.

"So," he started again after Chewy had a sip of his water, "what have you come for?"

"The resurrection flower," Chewy stated firmly.

The man lifted his eyebrows as if to ask, "That's all?"

Chewy shifted his head around, finding all the

flower girls gathered around them.

"Don't feel nervous, my friend," Halla-kkungi said, lowering his eyebrows. "We don't have visitors often, especially nowadays. Not too many people believe in this stuff anymore."

Chewy noted a hint of sadness in his voice before Halla-kkungi batted his eyes to regain his cheer.

"While you're here," he said, standing up, "why not a brief tour?"

Chewy scrunched up his mouth, not knowing how to express his next thought politely.

"I'm kind of in a rush," he mumbled.

"A short tour then—one that ends with the resurrection flower. Good?"

Chewy shrugged. It would have to do, and he hopped to his feet as Halla-kkungi moved into the sunlight.

"I took this garden over from my father, so I can guarantee you each flower does exactly as promised."

Each flower? How many different powers were there?

Before Chewy got the question out, Halla-kkungi pointed to a patch of purple blossoms to his left.

"These are the famous laughter flowers. One sight will leave any person laughing. Even hours afterward, they'll still have the giggles."

Chewy bent down looking at the small buds and full blossoms, but not a tiny part of him broke out in laughter.

"I don't think they're working," Chewy muttered, flicking one with his finger as if it were broken.

"Oh, of course not!" his guide chirped. "Their powers only become potent after being picked. Right now, they are as harmless as any other plant. If what you thought were true, these next flowers would've been responsible for far too many of my girls' deaths."

Chewy looked over to a bundle of red-spotted black petals. Behind them sat a sign with two large Chinese characters. Luckily, Chewy remembered his Hanja well enough to know what the sign said. Assassin flowers. He swallowed hard, picturing what they could do as his guide continued on.

"I used them once, when I was getting revenge for the death of my mother," he said, and Chewy glared up at him in surprise as he told more. "My enemies killed each other at the sight of it."

He lowered his head ashamed. Chewy felt bad and quickly tried to change the subject. "So how many different flowers are there?"

Forgetting his past deeds, the man shifted his eyes up, calculating. "More than three thousand. Some we've never even documented, afraid what their powers might be."

Chewy looked over the rippling rows of flowers. The possibilities of powers and unknown forces left Chewy's mind blank. It was the first time in his life that he had ever been so filled with curiosity that he couldn't move an inch.

"Now," Halla-kkungi said, snapping Chewy out of his reverie, and pulled a bag out of his pocket. "In order to bring your desired flower home, or any flower for that matter, you will need to keep it hidden from sight in this bag."

He pointed over to a small patch of pink flowers behind them and continued, "The resurrection flower is particularly a challenge. With one viewing, the dead will return, but should someone living see it, they will instantly die. It is rather strange, and not too many flowers possess such a double effect."

Chewy smiled. He loved when things worked out this way—making things a little bit more fun. Then something occurred to him. Maybe there was something here that could fix all of his problems, and thinking this, he touched his scar.

"You wouldn't by chance have a flower that makes you lucky or smart by looking at it, would you?"

The man twisted up his face, dropping his finger up and down as if flipping the pages of a book. He then lowered his vision back down to Chewy who could already tell what the answer was.

"Unfortunately not," he started, but reading the disappointment on Chewy's face quickly said, "That's not to say there isn't. As I said, there are many unknown flowers. Would you like to see some?"

Chewy could tell the man really wanted him to stay. As he said before, they didn't get visitors often, but Chewy knew he had little time and shook his head.

He was about to apologize and explain further his need for leaving when the man's head lifted, and his eyes sparkled with joy.

"Well, well, two visitors in one day! It is truly astounding!"

Two visitors?

Chewy turned around with a confused look and saw Gangnim step into the garden, his sword drawn. Gangnim's eyes darted around distrustfully at all the flower girls who had once again stopped with their watering to stare at the new visitor.

Chewy responded to the flower warden's amazement without taking his eyes off Gangnim's dark shadow. "I hate to disappoint you…but I'm pretty sure he's not here for the tour."

And at that moment, Gangnim spotted him, and Chewy felt an icy wave run over his skin. Things had just gotten a little bit harder.

18
Scapegoats

-Su Bin-

With the beeps of the keypad, Su Bin and Clint heard the lock slide open and play a little tune inviting them to enter. She had explained to him on the bus ride over that Chewy's father wouldn't be around. During the week, he stayed in another city, working on site in a lab for his company. Chewy's family was what Koreans called a weekend couple.

They stepped into the entrance, and before Clint could take a step further, she grabbed his shoulder, eyeing the shoes still on his feet. He blushed as he slipped them off, and both stepped onto the cold floor. The night sky outside the window made it hard to see.

"The light switch is on the other wall. Just a minute," she said, traipsing across the dark apartment, and then decided to take advantage of their time alone. "Tell me the truth now—what's going on between you two?"

She had hoped to get it out of him on the way over, almost tried once or twice on the swaying night bus, but she knew Clint felt nervous. And he had a right to. The entire ride over, everyone stared at them. It really wasn't their fault. Foreigners usually garnered attention, and it wasn't everyday people got to see one with metal pipes running up and down his legs. One boy even subtly asked his mother if Clint was Ironman. Su Bin was happy Clint didn't understand, but she blushed anyways.

With the light now on, Clint hemmed and hawed a bit to her question, shuffling his feet around for warmth before he spoke.

"I can't seem to explain it without it coming out all wrong," he said, but Su Bin looked at him with patient eyes, prodding him on. "Since Chewy lost his power, I've been trying to make him realize he has to change." He paused, closing his eyes as if about to jump off a large building and then resumed. "I admit I probably went about it in the wrong way."

He went on to explain to her how he had used Chewy's weakness in order to open Chewy's eyes. Unfortunately, this method rarely worked with people, and Clint seemed to know that now.

"He always pushes it off, pretending there's nothing wrong by saying, 'I've always had my confidence and done fine.' But he can't see that there is a problem because he refuses to face it. He helps everyone else with their problems, pointing them out as soon as possible, but for some reason, when it comes to the great Chewy Noh, he's not willing to talk about or even face up to his own."

Su Bin nodded her head. She knew exactly what he meant.

"He's very Korean that way," she said, and noticing Clint's furrowed brow as they moved into the kitchen, she quickly toned in with an explanation.

"Now I'm not saying all Koreans are that way," she started, putting her hands up to insinuate herself. "But Korea as a whole, quite often, likes to look the other way when it comes to its own problems."

"That's not too strange," Clint said. "America does it all the time. People saying this is wrong, and that we should fix it. That's what freedom of speech is."

Su Bin shook her head. It was a little bit more than that.

"In Korea, many times if you don't back the government, you're called a 'bal-gangy,'" she said scrunching up her face, trying to find an English equivalent. "It's kinda like saying you're a communist or something."

"Again, that happens in America too. Freedom-hater and stuff," Clint responded, taking a chair at the kitchen table.

"But in America, people pay attention. In Korea, the government just dismisses that there's anything wrong. My parents don't talk about it so much," she said, lowering her head out of shame, knowing her parents were a part of the problem. "But I've heard Chewy's parents rant on before. They've even gotten into fights with my parents a couple of times."

They both sat silent for a second, staring at each other. Su Bin wanted to desperately express to him how she felt, how frustrating it was to love her country and know it didn't care enough to be truthful to itself in order to fix its own problems.

It made her recall an incident from the year before. A major accident had happened, and had the government looked at things in a genuine way, they'd have seen it was due to corruption, not the scapegoat they soon concocted.

Before leaving, a transportation boat was found to be overloaded, but receiving some money, government inspectors overlooked it, letting the boat leave which resulted in the deaths of over a hundred students. In the wake of this tragedy, the government scrambled to protect itself, hunting down the boat company's ridiculously rich owner with claims of his enterprise being run like a mafia. With it, any mention of the government's fault for not having tougher regulations or control over bribery were washed aside. If anyone did mention it, they were criticized for hating their country.

Su Bin's eyes began to water as she couldn't understand how pointing out a country's mistakes in order to fix them, in hopes to improve the land they lived in, could be considered anti-patriotic.

Before her tears came, she noticed Clint's eyes frozen on something beside her, and she looked down, seeing a glowing phone. She glanced back with shock at Clint and quickly snatched the phone up, opening it. She listened to most of the messages before setting it back.

"It's his phone," she said, insinuating Chewy's grandfather. "All my messages are there…unchecked."

Clint dropped his head. "This means he hasn't even been back for the past two weeks. Do you think something really happened to him?"

Su Bin shrugged, feeling tears return to her eyes, knowing that this only meant Chewy was a step closer to death, and then she heard something.

Catching the white color of Clint's face, she knew he had heard it, too. She put her finger to her lips, and they heard it again.

"It sounded like a door closing," she whispered.

Clint nodded as Su Bin shouted out a "Hello?" that made him stiffen his back as if made of stone.

"What are you doing?" he said, his breath coming out in gasps.

"Trying to figure out who it is."

She turned to the hall next to the kitchen, and both heard the patter of feet darting into another room. Someone else was definitely there.

She waved her hand at him to not move as she stood up. She knew Clint wasn't the bravest boy in the world, and in that way, she was happy she'd have a chance to be in Chewy's shoes for once, slipping to the hall to see. And immediately, her voice left her.

At the end of the hall stood a large man with a black hat and wispy clothes. Having gotten a description of the creature that had killed Kent, she knew this to be another one just like it.

She turned to Clint and screamed, "Run!"

19
The remark that changes my mind

-Chewy-

"He's kinda with me," Chewy muttered to the flower warden without breaking eye contact with Gangnim who was now stalking through the rows in his direction.

"A friend of yours?" Halla-kkungi said, but Chewy could hear the doubt in his voice.

"Not exactly. He's just…doing his job." Chewy glanced at the uplifted and worried brow of the man next to him, and continued, "Don't worry. Everything will be fine, but I might need that."

He reached out, snagging the bag from the flower warden's loose grip and began walking backwards as Gangnim broke through the first domed shadow, coming within feet of where Chewy stood.

"It wasn't supposed to be this way," Gangnim intoned.

"Sorry about that," Chewy started. "Bigger things to take care of."

Saying this, he reached down, plucking a resurrection flower and tossed it in the bag. Now, all he'd have to do is get around Gangnim, which was clearly easier said than done.

"You know if there were some other way...I would," Gangnim said, placing both hands on his sword. "But as of now, it's Wednesday on Earth. You've had your time, and you wasted it on petty adventures instead of getting your things in order. I can't afford anymore delays."

Gangnim took a step forward to which Chewy lifted his free hand like a stop sign.

"You're not like the rest of them. I know that."

Gangnim stopped. Chewy could see something like confusion wrinkle over the shadowy face under the large helmet. He saw he had the large man's attention and continued. "I know a lot about you."

To this, Gangnim snorted. "What do you know about me?"

"I know you've taken orders all your life. That you wouldn't be here now if you knew the difference between when you should listen and when you shouldn't."

Chewy took another step backward and plucked a second flower from a different patch, setting it in his bag. He had come up with a plan, and in order for it to work, he needed a little time...and some luck, if he had any left.

"Is that so?" said Gangnim with a smirk, taking a step forward as Chewy retreated.

"If you hadn't listened to your king, the king of Gwa-yang, you'd never have become Death's messenger. You would never have lost your wife."

He caught Gangnim strangely lowering his head with a chuckle. Seeing his chance, Chewy picked two more buds from either side of the aisle before moving further back. He could already feel the weight in the bag, having gathered at least four different flowers. A couple more was all he needed.

"I've done a little digging into your past as well since the last we met," Gangnim said.

Chewy glared at him. What did that mean? He recalled the story of Samani and knew Gangnim could be tricky as well. Chewy wasn't going to fall for it.

All Chewy needed was one moment of weakness. Otherwise, he knew all too well the legend of Gangnim's mastery with a sword. If Gangnim was rational, Chewy had no chance.

"It's not going to work," Chewy barked back, tossing another two buds into his sack. "The past is done, for both of us! But you have a choice now! Will you see the mistakes you've made and change, or ignore them, only to repeat them again and again?"

After saying it, Chewy paused a bit. It seemed these words weren't just meant for Gangnim. Something inside himself reacted, too, but he pushed it aside for the time being as Gangnim lowered his sword slightly as if reviewing. In that instant, Chewy saw his chance.

He grabbed the first flower his hand found in the bag and tossed it in front of Gangnim, turning his own eyes away. He wasted no time figuring out what happened and darted down the aisle, following the outer wall of the garden to keep his distance from where he knew Gangnim was. It wasn't till he made it to the front gate that he decided to look back and was surprised at what he saw.

Gangnim lay on the ground, rolling with laughter, his sword off to the side. Chewy smiled, waving to the stunned flower warden as he dashed through the gate back into the woods.

Treading down the dirt path, he held the bag full of unknown flowers tightly. He couldn't wait to get home to discover what little treasures he had picked. But in the back of his mind, something clicked together. With his little speech to Gangnim, Chewy realized there was a lot of thinking he had to do. And it all revolved around his scar.

20
I made a mistake

-Su Bin-

Luckily, the strange man in the hall wasn't very fast moving, and Su Bin was able to dash through the kitchen with Clint onto the back veranda where Chewy's family hung their wet clothes. Both lowered down to not be seen through the window in the top of the door, and they tried to control their breathing as they huffed from shock and exertion.

The veranda, like all Korean verandas, was poorly insulated and so with the colder night air, their breath came out in hot puffs. Su Bin with her skinny body began to shiver, having left her coat at the front door. Seeing this, Clint took his off, draping it around her.

"No, no," she whispered, pushing her arms open for him to take the coat back, causing him to hug her tightly as she protested, "You'll be cold too."

He nodded. "Yes, but…I'll be okay."

She saw the warmth in his eyes and smiled, forgetting for a second that a killer wraith was stalking around inside Chewy's house.

With her eyes still on him, Clint continued. "I want to say something,"

At the sound of a door slamming within, they both jerked their heads to the window before Clint repeated himself to get her attention again. "I don't know what's going to happen next, so I just wanted you to know because, you know, I tend to be quite, well, afraid and not brave to do things and—"

Su Bin cut him off with a sharp whisper. "Just tell me what it is!"

Clint closed his eyes, swallowing hard.

"I like you," he said and opening his eyes to Su Bin's face, didn't seem satisfied with her reaction, so added, "What I mean is I like like you."

To this, Su Bin's eyes turned back into tiny slits. With those words, her whole body rippled with warmth, and her fingers tingled. She tried to respond but found her head was overwhelmed with a delightful numbness.

And at that moment, as both were distracted, the door next to them swung open, and they saw the dark caped man standing there with his sword drawn. Su Bin's mouth dropped open, seeing the glint of moonlight on the blade. She wanted to scream and reach out for Clint's hand but before she could, the dark man lunged forward, driving the blade through Clint's chest. Su Bin watched it pierce Clint's shirt in slow-motion, ripping out the backside of him. She felt as if her own heart was being cut as Clint bent forward onto the blade, his eyes wide, staring at her for help, and then he slid backwards off the sword to the ground.

She quickly tossed her head up to the scowling face, fully expecting herself to be next, but the dark man just stopped with a perplexed look, scrunching up its nose. He bounced his head from side to side as if looking for something or someone else and, not finding it, turned, closing the door behind him.

Su Bin was frozen and stared at the door, not believing what had just happened. She heard the man's footsteps move away from the kitchen and disappear, and only then did she turn to Clint's pale face and limp body.

She put a hand on his cold cheek. Tears were already welling up in her eyes. She touched his chest, finding no wound or even hole in his shirt but knew he was dead. Her cheeks grew red as she tried fighting back the tears, and she struggled to get her next words out in a strained whisper.

"I like like you, too."

And she dropped her head down, sobbing. After a couple of minutes, she lifted her tear-lined face. She was ready to move on now. It was time to do something about it.

-Chewy's Grandmother-

Chewy's grandmother was standing in the hall outside Chewy's room, staring at the hall closet. She couldn't understand it. Somehow Chewy's mom had missed it—the fact that there was something else here. Why? She didn't know. She had seen it instantly, coming back from the hardware store but decided to keep it quiet from Chewy and Clint. Somehow, she felt it fit into all her assumptions, and she didn't want to spoil the surprise. The less people that knew meant a chance at a better outcome, and she was going to need as many cards up her sleeve as possible.

Touching the handle to the closet, she heard the phone ring in the kitchen and dashed out there, stopping to look at it. Who could be calling now? The sky was getting dark as evening sank in. With Chewy gone, there was no reason for a call, but she instantly sensed it was important, and picked up. Immediately, she heard Su Bin's frantic voice over the line.

"Auntie?"

"No, it's me," she said, hoping this was enough explanation for the girl. She didn't want to openly admit she was the spirit of Chewy's dead grandmother. In that second, she heard a sob and knew something was wrong.

"What is it?" she asked.

She heard Su Bin swallow hard on the other end before responding. "One of those things was here—"

"Where?"

"In Chewy's house—here in Korea, it—"

None of this made sense, and she cut Su Bin off again. "What was it doing there?"

"It killed Clint!" she screamed, and Chewy's grandmother drew the phone away from her ear.

Clint was in Korea?

She shook her head. What did Chewy have planned? She rubbed her forehead before drawing the phone back to her ear to speak.

"Now, listen to me, Su Bin," she said with a tough voice. She needed the girl to calm down. "If we can get his body back here, when Chewy returns with the resurrection flower, we can fix everything. But we need him back here. Is there anyway you can do that?"

She heard silence for a second as if Su Bin were thinking.

"I don't think so. The bridge is back in my apartment…across town. I don't know what to do."

The mu-dang scratched her chin. There had to be a way, and then she thought of something, running back to the closet door as she spoke.

"Su Bin, you have to come back here alone first. I will give you an incantation to bring back there in order to build a door bridge to this house. Can you do that?"

This time, she knew the pause she heard was for another reason, and finally Su Bin answered.

"I already have an incantation," she whimpered.

Chewy's grandmother stiffened up. "You already have one? How?"

"Clint brought it…said Chewy wanted him to do something with it."

That boy! Why did he always have to do things behind her back? She gritted her teeth to hold in her frustration but realized, in this instance, his secrets were actually going to help them out.

"That's fine, Su Bin," she responded, holding back the anger in her voice. "Put it on a door there."

She looked up at the closet in front of her and then quickly spat out another command.

"Put it on the closet door in Chewy's room," she said, smirking. Things were beginning to make sense. "I will do the ritual here to connect the doors in order for you to get back but remember both of you must be in the room when I do it, so make sure to drag his body in there. Got it?"

She heard a sad, squeaky "yes," and then put the phone down.

Five minutes later, having completed the ritual, she stepped into the newly made door bridge. She was excited in a way. She hadn't seen Korea since she died.

-*Susie*-

The sky was growing darker around her, and

Susie knew she should go home soon. Even though the days were warm, the nights still snipped at exposed noses and fingers. She could already see her breath fogging up in front of her face, but Susie couldn't stop staring at the yellow house across the street.

She had watched lights go on and off in it for over thirty minutes, catching the image of Chewy's mom dashing around from room to room. At one point, she even saw her dressed in some rainbow like costume. Chewy definitely had a strange family.

But for the past five minutes, she had seen nothing, which didn't bother her. What did bother her was that she had yet to see Chewy anywhere. Was Chewy actually sick or did this have something to do with Kent being missing, on top of the strange illnesses that had beset his mother and those other students earlier that year?

Her curiosity grew as if someone had whispered a thousand questions into her ear with the early spring wind. She had to know what was going on in that house, and she stepped into the street, crossing the road to find out.

His lawn was mushy, so she followed the sidewalk up to the door and rang the bell.

No answer.

She knocked as loudly as she could, only to get the same response.

This made her worry. Hadn't she just seen Chewy's mom? She decided this warranted more extreme action, and she grabbed the handle to the door, finding it unlocked.

"Chewy?" she yelled, pushing the door open enough to stick her head in.

The house sat silent as she darted her head around the kitchen and living room. Wasn't his mom just here?

Susie walked into the house, closing the door behind her. She repeated his name a couple more times before braving the hallway.

With the darkening sky, the house took on an eerie feeling, and the thought of something jumping out to get her crossed her mind more than once.

Reaching Chewy's bedroom, she looked in and froze in her footsteps at what she saw. How could this be? There must be some explanation for it, but none of it made sense.

21
Mistakes Revealed

-Chewy-

Chewy found the return trip took less time, despite it taking half a year. He had a lot to think about, and this kept his mind distracted. On top of that, he was pushing himself hard. He knew the laughing flower wouldn't hold Gangnim off for long, and his house was the best bet. It was the only place he was protected.

So he was expecting to feel relieved, stepping through the fridge door back into his kitchen, hoping to see a waiting Clint, if not his grandmother. Instead, what he saw was overwhelming.

Screams and a low crying poured out from the living room, and looking over, he saw Su Bin rocking back and forth in the corner. In front of her was Clint's limp, pale body. He didn't need an explanation. He was pretty sure he could piece together what had happened, especially since Su Bin was wearing Clint's coat—the one he had put the protective pin in.

Next to Su Bin, his grandmother petted Su Bin's back, trying to calm her, but stood up straight with a mixed expression on her face upon seeing him. Chewy saw part of it was anger, but with the wailing Su Bin in the room, he knew also that, for her sake, he was going to be spared a reprimanding.

"You have the flower?" his grandmother spit out.

"Sort of," he said, lowering his head.

"What do you mean?"

Chewy opened his eyes wide at the scene, recalling his journey. It was a lot to take in, but he tried to explain. "Kinda ran into Gangnim."

His grandmother's eyes widened in shock, and Chewy patted his body. "I'm fine. Look!"

Seeing her relax, he lifted the bag. "In order to get away, I had to pick some extra flowers to slow him down. One of these is the resurrection flower…I just don't know which one."

Su Bin's crying had subsided for the moment, and his grandmother helped her to the couch, picking up where she had left off with rubbing her back, and said, "As you can see, your little secret has caused some unnecessary problems."

Chewy's face turned red. He was about to bring up the many secrets of hers, but she cut him off before he could do so.

"Right now's not the time," she said holding up her free hand. "I had to make a door bridge to

Korea just to get them back here."

As she said this, she pointed to the hall, and Chewy tossed his head over, catching sight of the linen closet. Not exactly as he had planned, but in the end, it may work out anyways.

He walked into the room further and lowered to get Su Bin's attention.

"It'll be alright," he said, reaching out for his cousin's knee to console her. "I'm here now, and we'll get everything back to normal. Don't worry."

Su Bin glanced upward, her eyes swollen and red. She nodded but couldn't get a word out. Looking over at his grandma, he then realized there was something else.

"What?" he asked.

His grandma looked away before answering. "That's what I was trying to explain to you. We ran into another snag while we were out."

Chewy leaned forward, nodding to get one of them to continue, but only saw both look to the living room wall that lined his bedroom. He stood up, following their gaze until it dawned on him, and he ran to his room.

Standing in the hall with the door wide open, he saw why they were acting weird. Kent's body was gone. He tossed his head back down the hall to them. "You can't be serious?"

The silence from the living room answered everything.

He dove to the floor and scrambled across it to

look under the beds. But there was no body, and he dashed back out into the living room.

"Where is he?"

Su Bin dropped her head as his grandmother spoke up. "We don't exactly know. It was there before I made the door bridge, but when we got back…"

Chewy looked from face to face before asking, "So what does this mean?"

His grandmother shook her head. "Unfortunately, the resurrection flower doesn't work unless we have a body. We can save your friend here, but the other boy…it doesn't look good."

Chewy lowered his eyes, feeling defeated. His whole trip was for nothing, and what Clint said had come true. Here Clint was now, lying dead at his feet. Chewy couldn't help but think that maybe if he had listened, none of this would have happened.

"There's no other way?" he asked with a supplicating tone.

"Without a body…it'd take nothing less than going down to the underground to bring him back yourself. And that is out of the question," she said, her voice dropping at the end to signify the serious impossibility of it.

Seeing the worry on Chewy's face, Su Bin looked up at him and spoke. "I'm sorry, Chewy. It's all our fault."

Chewy shook his head.

"There's nothing we can do about it now," he said.

Suddenly, his grandmother stood up, rubbing her forehead, moaning. Su Bin jumped to her side, asking what was wrong.

"Looks like I have some more bad news," she said, staring at Chewy. "Your mom seems to be trying to get control of her body again. So, maybe, it'd be best if I lie down or something for a while."

She moved slowly to the hall before looking back at them.

"She's the last thing we need, and I think I should be able to hold her back for the time being. Meanwhile, you guys get to work," she said and lifted her eyes to Chewy to say, "But, please, hurry."

Chewy raised an eyebrow. He couldn't believe how reasonable she was being. Maybe she had changed. Maybe she was finally seeing he could do some things by himself. Now, he only had to hope for the same from his mom, and he nodded to his grandmother as she left.

Turning to Su Bin, Chewy was happy to have her back in America with him and quickly remembered something.

"What day is it? How long have I been gone?"

She scrunched up her tiny nose.

"I don't know. This is American time. In Korea, it's Thursday. According to Clint," she said, pausing for a moment to look at his body with wet eyes before finishing, "he said you left two days ago."

Chewy did the math, and that meant Gangnim was telling the truth. Today was his death day—only two days had passed—even though his trip had felt like over a year or so of walking.

"So…what next?" she squeaked.

Chewy shook his head. It was a long list.

"We find Kent's body, and then my grandfather to fix this curse," he said. "But first, we see what we can do to get Clint here back from the dead."

22
How My Grandfather Became A POW

-Joong Bum-

Most people don't know this, but most of the land won and lost in the war happened within the first six months. The other two and a half years were spent arguing over the treaty.

The North started strong, sweeping down to Busan in astonishing speed; they reached the harbor city in almost six weeks. It then took the South, led by the Americans, only three weeks to gain it all back before beginning their push toward the Northern capital. At the four-month mark, China joined, thwarting our hopes, and began their thrust back to where it started along the 38th parallel. It was at this point that everything changed for me.

Jeong and I with the rest of our battalion were stationed on a mountain pass in Northern territory. There had been gunfire for a couple of days, but our reports were to stay still. It wasn't until late that afternoon in a cool fall breeze that we saw the first Chinese troops break free of the opposite ridge.

Our captain immediately barked orders, and we bunkered down as bullets began whizzing by. We all felt overwhelmed. The sea of soldiers flying toward us didn't stop. It was the Chinese and their human-wave attack. We were easily outnumbered.

Before they were even upon us, the soldier to my left—a boy only a year or two older than me—broke down crying. However, for the most part, the rest of us kept our heads, shooting off into the distance.

Soon their artillery struck the ground around us, tossing up dirt, clogging the air and our vision. The Chinese soldiers stomping toward us looked like ghosts, zipping over the earth to reap our souls.

We fired unendingly, knowing there was no chance for retreat. They would only hunt us down and shoot us in the back. The explosions grew, and so did the screams of soldiers next to me. I just stayed level, firing into the dust at anything that moved, and then it was as if a crack of thunder silenced everything.

I turned my head and saw all the others moving in slow motion, and a red blast flooded my eyesight. After that I didn't remember much.

When I opened my eyes again, the world was complete darkness. For a second, I thought I was dead, but it didn't make sense. I could feel my arms and my legs. I just couldn't move. Wiggling my torso, I realized someone lay on top of me, and I slid my hands beneath the body, heaving it to the side.

With it gone, the dust began to clear, and I found myself with thirteen Chinese soldiers staring down at me. Their guns were leveled on my head.

In that moment, I thought it was all over. I wondered how my mother would take the news. I almost hoped she'd never hear of it. It would only crush her. Later, I found that to be true. I've had nightmares of her death ever since returning to Korea. I wish no one to ever live through something similar.

But, with all the guns on me, I was not killed. Another soldier jumped down into the hole I was in and helped me up. Seeing I was okay, he pointed over to the next hole, saying something in Chinese that I didn't understand. Seeing my confusion, he grabbed my hand dragging me up with him.

I stood at the edge of the next hole, and my face turned white. I saw Jeong's head covered in blood and almost turned away to throw up when Jeong began coughing. He was alive!

I jumped inside with the Chinese soldier and began digging. With the blast that had knocked me out, Jeong's hole had collapsed, pinning his legs under a pile of dirt. At that moment, I understood what the Chinese soldier had said to me. He wanted help digging out my friend.

We worked for a good twenty minutes before uncovering enough to free him, but the job was only harder after that. Jeong's legs had been buried for so long that they had lost blood circulation. They'd be okay eventually, but right then, he wasn't able to walk, so both the Chinese soldier and I strained ourselves to lift him.

With Jeong out of the hole, we gave him water and tried massaging the blood back down to his legs. Soon Jeong moved his toes. And the soldier and I grabbed each other, jubilant at our accomplishment.

With his arm around me, the Chinese soldier patted me on the back, and looking into my face, smiled, flashing a thumbs-up in my direction. To this day, I still can't comprehend it. Only minutes before, this man was a part of the barrage that killed every other soldier in our battalion. He had wanted us dead as sure as we had wanted the same for him. But somehow, as soon as the bullets stopped flying, we ended up on the same side, trying to help whatever injured we found. I will never understand what this thing 'war' is. I don't know how anyone could.

Soon after, we began marching back with a small group to their camp. The other soldiers left behind started digging in for the next round of attacks. I felt sorry for them only because I was done for now.

Within a couple hours of walking, Jeong and I arrived at a small outpost. Most of the buildings looked beat up, but there were soldiers mulling around everywhere. The soldier that pulled me out helped Jeong to a particularly gray building. He muttered something in Chinese, tipped his head to both of us, and left. I never saw him again.

Inside was a hospital, and upon entering, Jeong and I were led to a room with four beds. We took the two on one side while two wounded Chinese soldiers occupied the other.

The staff of the hospital treated everyone equally, whether Chinese or South Korean. One moment that particularly stood out in my head was when a bombing raid had occurred during our stay. One part of the hospital collapsed, and in that moment, everyone worked together, enemies side by side to help the injured. Not once did Jeong or I think otherwise. We were away from the frontline, which meant humans were humans, and those hurt needed help.

Then, three weeks later, we left. Our wounds were mostly surface ones, and getting cleared by the doctors, we were shipped out to join the rest of the POWs.

The Chinese surge had already been going on when we were caught. In this way, we were lucky. Those caught in the first waves had the worst time. Despite trying to comply with the treatment of POWs according to the Geneva Convention, the Chinese were unprepared for so many POWs at the rate they collected them. They had to march many further south to camps that had yet been built. Many POWs died along the way.

Getting to the camp, Jeong and I encountered much hardship even though conditions were better compared to the first part of the war. We were questioned heavily, asked many times to repeat our answers or come in for interviews that went over the same questions. If we produced wrong answers, or ones that did not match our previous ones, we were detained longer. However, I often heard the American and British troops had it much worse than us Koreans.

The Chinese didn't trust them, nor did the North Koreans. It was their goal to break their spirits, whether with violence or brainwashing. In this way, every morning, all of us POWs were paraded outside to listen to daily reports and speeches about the great life in Communist China. Their stories described a world of rich, happy people where problems never seemed to spring up.

I can understand how the Chinese must've grown frustrated. None of this ridiculousness worked. Most soldiers said what they had to in order to be left alone. But no one was buying it.

Soon, reports of double agents surfaced. Supposedly, certain POWs working as Chinese operatives were spreading false information around in hopes of luring some to their side. With this, there were sudden 'peace' groups started by unknown POWs declaring America should just leave Korea alone. But in the end, all of it was nothing more than rumors. I never witnessed any of the above events.

For this reason, we POWs had distrust for any type of news. Everything around us was propaganda, making it impossible to know what the truth was or wasn't. The height of the Chinese / North Korean propaganda machine came roughly nine months after my capture with the announcement of an Inter-camp Olympic Games.

These games would bring about the end of everything.

Part III: Earth

23
Tests

-Chewy-

The sky was fully dark by the time Chewy and Su Bin had carried Clint's body into his bedroom. They figured it was better to have him in eyesight for what they had to do next. One missing body was enough.

Chewy collapsed on his bed, as did Su Bin, leaving Clint lifeless by the closet. Both of them were small and not used to carrying something so long and awkward. After catching his breath, Chewy sat up, eyeing the bag of flowers on the desk next to him. Now all they had to do was discover which flower did what. While moving Clint, they had agreed on how to do it.

Since the flowers only affected the person who saw them, they would take turns picking out of the sack while the other kept their eyes shut. Doing so, they'd report what each one did and then put it in a separate bag labeled with a number. Chewy knew there were at least six left after he used the laughing one on Gangnim.

Su Bin finally sat up, looking exhausted. Her eyes were still a little swollen, and Chewy sensed it wasn't just stress. Something had happened between her and Clint in his Korean apartment. But he filed it away for later, focusing on the task at hand.

"You ready?" he said, picking the bag up.

She nodded. Su Bin had insisted on going first, for Clint's sake.

Chewy extended the bag out to her, and snapped his eyes shut as tight as he could get them. He didn't want to make a mistake. If she pulled out the resurrection flower on the first draw, it meant she would die, and he didn't want to accidentally see it too, leaving a room full of dead bodies for when his mom woke up.

"Here goes," Su Bin said, and Chewy felt a tug at the bag.

For the first couple of seconds, nothing happened. Chewy waited for some kind of response, almost ready to call out to her when he heard the springs on her bed compress. He couldn't believe it—were they that lucky to have found it on the first pick?

"Su Bin," he said, reaching out with a free hand. She was flat on the bed. He shook her but there was no movement. She seemed pretty dead.

He traced his fingers along her, locating her empty hands. She must have dropped the flower to the floor. If he could cover it up, then he would be able to inspect her better.

Patting the ground, eventually he felt the soft petals and quickly placed it in one of the bags on the desk. In that instant, he heard a yawn and opening his eyes, saw Su Bin fluttering her lids as she sat up.

"What happened?" she asked.

Chewy scrunched his face up, looking at the bag. This didn't make sense. The flower warden had said if it were the resurrection flower, she'd have to take another look at it in order to be revived, not just simply cover it up.

"I don't know," he said. "What did it feel like?"

She drowsily licked her lips and said, "I think…I think I was dreaming."

He looked to the bag in his hand. No wonder he thought he found the resurrection flower. Didn't they say death was just the big sleep?

"I'm pretty sure that was a sleeping flower," he announced.

"That explains why I feel so groggy," she said, stretching her tiny arms. "So, you're next."

Chewy gulped. He was expecting this to be fun but hoped there wasn't an exploding flower that made whomever see it bust apart into pieces. There was probably no coming back from that one.

"Ready," he said, handing the big bag over to her and saw her snap her tiny eyes shut.

He reached into the bag, feeling the cold brush of petals, exhaled heavily, and yanked one out.

At first, nothing happened. Chewy squinted, wondering if he had to look at it in a certain way to make it work. Eventually, Su Bin spoke up.

"What's going on?"

"Nothing," he said, "I think we have a dud."

Su Bin opened one eye slowly and not seeing anything wrong, relaxed.

"It doesn't look broken," she said.

"It's not like either of us would know," Chewy added, lifting it up higher so both could see. "When have we ever gotten flowers—though I'm sure you wouldn't mind some from Clint."

"I would love flowers from Clint," she gushed and then stood up straight with an embarrassed look on her face.

Chewy stared at her. "What?"

Her eyes were big while answering. "I didn't want to say that. It…just sort of came out. I was thinking it, and my mouth…said it."

Chewy lowered his eyebrows.

"You don't think…" he started and saw the "what?" expression on Su Bin's face before finishing, "It's a truth flower?"

Su Bin's mouth hung open before saying, "Only one way to find out." She gulped and then said, "Before this past winter, did you hate me?"

Chewy couldn't see how this proved anything. She already knew this. Nonetheless, his mouth started moving. "Yes."

He shook his head. How did that happen?

"And if I had died, how would you have felt?"

He looked at her. What was she getting at? But again, his mouth opened. "I would've been unbelievably happy."

Saying this, he clapped his hands over his mouth. This was a little scary, and he quickly added, "But that's not how I feel now. I didn't want to say that. I promise! I didn't—"

She lifted a finger, cutting him off.

"When you get back to Korea," she started, and he could see her eyes turning red again, "will we still be close?"

Lifting one eyebrow up, he leaned back a bit, shocked. He had no idea this bothered her. He just thought she knew. This time he didn't even try to fight back the words.

"Of course. Why wouldn't we?"

She twisted her head around, but there was no way she could hold it back.

"My mom," she mumbled.

Chewy nodded. He knew what Su Bin's family was like, and her mom was the worst. He recalled many punishments dealt out to him for bad manners or impolite speaking. Su Bin's mom was a stickler to the old ways. This was one reason Chewy didn't see his cousin as often as he could.

"I'm not going anywhere. No matter what anyone else says or thinks," he added.

She looked at him. The brightness in her face had returned.

"Now, let's get saving your boyfriend," he said.

She turned red but with a smile, and he closed

his eyes.

The next flower took no time at all to realize what it was. As soon as it left the bag, Chewy heard and then smelled it. Before he even had time to speak, Su Bin had it in the bag numbered three while Chewy tried to hold back his laughter. Opening his eyes, he felt a gentle slap on his arm.

"What did you eat?" he said with a smile.

She stuck her lips out, pouting.

"I didn't fart," she said, wiggling back and forth. "The stupid flower made me."

They had lined the smaller bags in a row on the desk, and Chewy eyed the third one. He now knew what Clint was going to find in a wrapped box on his birthday and smiled, thinking of it.

"I hope you get something horrible," she said, snatching the bag away from Chewy and thrust it forward for him to pick from.

He put his left hand on her shoulder, staring at her tightly shut eyes, and said, "After that, I don't think there's anything that can top it."

Then, Chewy dipped his hand in, happy he wouldn't have to go through what she just did, and as soon as he saw the tips of the flower pop out of the bag, he knew what it was.

And everything went black.

24
Stuck between a Rock and a Hard Place

-Chewy-

For the first couple minutes, there was only darkness. Chewy heard voices screaming and feet stomping, but his brain hadn't kicked in yet. Eventually, his eyes flickered and images appeared.

Everything had a gray tone to it, and there seemed to be pillars everywhere, shooting upward, disappearing into a strange fog. A faint red tint lit the air, making it all the more eerie. He pushed himself up off the ground to sit and looked around. There was no one in sight.

And then it dawned on him. This was the underground, and he scurried to his feet.

He hoped Su Bin would get him out of here soon without ending up dead herself, but until that happened, he knew he had to be careful. This was Gangnim's realm, and Chewy darted his head around at the slightest sound.

Though he expected Gangnim to come floating

through the mist, it was another figure altogether that took shape. The black hat didn't immediately tip Chewy off, nor did the red eyes, but the low moaning voice did the trick.

"Yeomra said you'd be down here soon enough," it said, smiling at the scar on Chewy's face as it came into view.

Chewy shuffled backwards, recognizing the ghost instantly, and held himself up against one of the rocky pillars. He arched his back in a defensive stance.

"Sorry to disappoint, but it's not my time yet," Chewy spit out, darting his eyes around for an escape path.

The large ghost lowered down, smoke lifting from the emptiness around its eyes.

"Take a look around. You're here, alright." It wrinkled its face into a gap-toothed smile. "All newbies like you think, 'No, it's not my turn,' but it is."

For a second, these words worked, and fear slithered up Chewy's backbone.

"No, that's not true. I have other things to do first," he said in protest, remembering faintly Su Bin and something above that had to be done.

The ghost entwined its fingers, happy with the moment that lay before it.

"You're here now—why fight it?" it said, and seeing Chewy lower his neck in confusion, it continued, "It's not like you're alone. Your friend is already down here, and now that you've joined him, it only means that the old mu-dang is left."

Mu-dang? He blinked rapidly trying to draw up thoughts. Things were coming back to him in fragments.

"I'll find a way—don't worry!" he blurted out at the creature.

It smiled again. "I'm so happy to see you haven't lost that confidence of yours. It makes this all the more rewarding."

Chewy leaned forward to speak but noticed nothing came from his throat. He grabbed it, trying to force his words out again, but it didn't work. His voice was gone, and then he felt lightheaded.

The specter's eyes grew large seeing this, and it thrust a hand forward. "No! You're supposed to stay! He said you'd be mine."

Its hand flew right through Chewy's body, but he didn't feel anything, and before he knew it, everything went black again, and he heard only a last few screams from the ghost.

"It's not fair!"

When Chewy came to again, Su Bin was crouched over him with her eyes shut, shaking him while she repeated his name over and over. He grabbed her hands to make her stop, and she froze, her voice dropping out.

"I'm back. Don't worry," he said, and then realized the flower was still in her other hand. "Don't open your eyes yet!"

He grabbed it from her and scurried on hands and knees over to Clint. He knew he couldn't close his eyes or blink. There was no way he was going back to that dark place. And to make sure of that, he had to revive Clint, no matter how dry his eyes got.

He tossed himself on Clint's body and thrust his fingers onto Clint's eyebrows, yanking up the eyelids. His own eyes had now begun to water over, and he knew he wouldn't be able to keep it this way for long. He stared past the flower in his hand to Clint's lifeless pupils, whispering, "come on," over and over.

Finally, Clint's chest uplifted violently as if his soul had shoved its way back into him, and Chewy tossed the flower under the bed to get it out of view. He blinked to clear his eyes out and soon saw Clint heaving next to the closet door. His face glowed red as if holding his breath for hours.

"You alright?" Chewy gasped.

At first, Clint didn't say anything. He just stared around him as if none of it made sense.

"Is this real?" he wheezed.

Su Bin came to his side, grabbing his hand. Chewy saw her eyes were reddening again.

"You're back," she said, trying to calm Clint down. "We got you back."

Clint looked up with wide eyes at Su Bin's face, and Chewy didn't know what it was, but something had happened to his best friend.

"What is it?" he asked.

As Clint's breathing slowed, the red left his face, and eventually, he spoke.

"It was so real...they," his voice went out as he imagined what he had seen. Clint started to shake. Chewy had seen this before. This was what happened whenever Clint's aquaphobia got the best of him.

Chewy jumped up, tearing the blanket from his bed to cover him. Wrapped securely, Clint was able to squeak out a little more.

"They were angry because they wanted you," he said, looking at Chewy. "The saja was in your apartment looking for you, not us. We were just unlucky."

Chewy gulped, and his own memory of the underground came back to him. From what the ghost said, his grandmother was in trouble too, and he leaped to his feet, moving for the door.

"Wait here!" he said and dashed down the hall to his mother's room, throwing the door wide. He stood in awe staring into it. Everything was there except for his grandmother.

"What's wrong?" Su Bin squeaked out from Chewy's bedroom.

"She's gone," he said in a low voice, and then rang out a little louder, "My grandmother is gone."

He headed back to his room, running over the past events in his head. There was no way they had gotten her. The ghost below was quite confident that she was next, which meant that they didn't have her yet, and that left only one other option: his grandmother was planning something. That had to be why she let them revive Clint alone. She would have never allowed them to do that, and he chided himself for not figuring it out earlier.

Coming back into the room, he kicked his bed in anger, letting out a slight scream of frustration.

Clint jumped, still nestled in the corner with Su Bin by his side, and she looked up to him and asked what was wrong.

He glared at his open door as his heart banged away inside. He felt overwhelmed…and alone.

"My grandmother's off doing her secret business again. My grandfather's disappeared, and Kent's body is gone!" He rubbed his face and said, "It just seems like every time I turn around another person is dead or missing! I'm just wondering when things are going to start going my way."

Chewy slid down the wall, sitting directly between the bed and Clint. He hunched over so that his eyes rested on the floor. At this moment, Clint's voice piped up.

"Kent's body is missing?"

Looking over, Chewy saw the color returning to his best friend's face and the hint of worry that always seemed to cheer him up. Maybe things weren't all bad.

"It happened while you were…dead," Chewy said, trying to soften the last part. He shrugged and gave Clint a fake smile. Whatever stress and problems he had were probably nothing compared to what Clint had just gone through, and Chewy refocused his brain. There had to be a way to fix everything.

He closed his eyes, dropping his head back against the wall.

"The resurrection flower is still under the bed," he said. "We'll have to get it if we ever find Kent's body."

Su Bin shuffled to her feet, sliding over to the edge of the bed with the bag, saying she'd get it. Chewy warned her to keep her eyes closed and turned to Clint.

"None of this is what I wanted," he said in lieu of apology.

Clint shifted over in Chewy's direction, saying, "You look…different? Is your hair longer?"

Chewy ran his hand over his head. It did feel longer. He wondered if this was an effect from the higher realms, but before he could figure it out, Su Bin's head popped up from the bed with a peculiar smile.

Both boys dropped their eyebrows, staring at her.

"What're you so happy about?" Chewy spit out.

"Because I know where to look next," she said, holding up a hair barrette between her thumb and pointer finger.

"The hair store?" Clint squeaked.

"No," she groaned. "I spent enough time with

Susie to know everything she has, and this is definitely one of her barrettes."

Chewy's eyes grew.

Now, they had something.

25
Escape During Sleep

-Chewy-

The next morning in the bathroom, Chewy studied himself in the mirror. He had definitely changed since going to the upper realms. Not only was his hair longer, his scar seemed more faded as if a great amount of time had passed. In a way, he was happy because it meant he was probably a good year older than Clint. But being a year older than his best friend wasn't enough to keep his worries away.

The night before, Su Bin and Clint left a little after ten o'clock. Clint's mom wasn't going to be a problem. They easily shoved it off on having a test to study for. Luckily too, this little adventure fell during sleeping hours in Korea, though Su Bin's excessive sleepiness the next day would be hard to explain.

Chewy pushed his hair around in the mirror, wondering if he needed it cut as he recalled the other events of the night. One in particular weighed heavily upon him.

After finding the barrette, they all fell into a circle in the middle of his room, the barrette in the center for all to see.

"How could Susie even get in here?" Clint asked incredulously, still wrapped in Chewy's bedspread.

"Doesn't matter," Su Bin started. "Unless you guys have invited her in here on some other occasion, I think this proves she was here."

Clint and Chewy looked at each other. There was no other explanation, but it did seem far-fetched. What would've provoked Susie to act now?

"I spent a lot of time with her when I was here," Su Bin continued, catching their questioning glances. "She was nice and...I needed someone like that—with confidence and everything. If you recall, neither of you were talking to me at the time. Still, that doesn't mean I didn't know what she was up to."

"Up to?" Chewy said with a lifted eyebrow.

"She never let on to me, but she was helping Kent get you whenever she had a chance."

Chewy gritted his teeth. He knew there had to be something. There was no way Kent was that smart—with or without his power.

He looked to Clint.

"It makes sense," Chewy said, hoping to clear it up for his friend. "She's been after me ever since I rejected her, last fall."

Clint let the covers slip down. There was something both he and Su Bin were missing.

"Are you saying Susie took Kent's body?" Clint asked.

Chewy glanced at Su Bin who too was dumbstruck for a second. That was what they were assuming, but with Clint saying it out loud, they both realized how insane it was. Before Chewy could get out another word, Su Bin jumped in.

"You're right. She probably didn't. Kent's much bigger than her. Besides, it'd be impossible for her to drag his body away without someone else seeing," she said, pausing for a second. "But, if anything, she may know what did happen."

They all lowered their heads in agreement. Despite this, they came up with little of how to resolve it. However, the next hour was not a complete waste. They did catch Clint up on everything he had missed while dead—the new door bridge in the hall being the most important.

By the time it got late, they ended on a high note, hoping that when Chewy's grandmother returned, she would be able to offer some advice. As it was, they had nothing. And that's when something unnerving happened.

After Clint and Chewy watched Su Bin leave through the bridge to Korea for a tiring day, Clint brushed by Chewy for the front door.

"Where are you going?" Chewy said with a look of confusion.

Clint opened the door.

"I'm walking home," he said, and the cool spring breeze that blew in caused both to shiver.

"What's wrong with the bridge?" Chewy said and shifted a thumb in his bedroom's direction.

"I was thinking after you said all those things earlier," he started, holding the door open. "Maybe I have to do something about it—maybe I have to start addressing my fear. No more door bridge for me…unless there's an emergency or something."

Clint was referring to their argument before Chewy went to the upper realms. It felt strange for Chewy only because it seemed to have happened ages ago.

"You know, when that happened, I didn't mean you had to run out and do this. I just needed you to act a little braver. That's all," Chewy said, lowering his eyes. He hoped none of this had hurt their friendship, and Clint spoke up.

"I'm not doing it because of that." He turned to leave, and then quickly looked back before stepping into the night. "I was kind of hoping it would make you think a little bit about yourself."

And, at that, he left.

Clint's last words echoed through Chewy's head the rest of the night. He tried making sense of them, but he didn't know where to start. What scared Chewy the most was that it wasn't an argument anymore. It was as if Clint was waving a white flag. Chewy never thought his best friend would give up on him, and it only made things harder.

On his trip home from the upper realms, Chewy hadn't wasted a moment. His physical appearance wasn't the only thing that came back altered. Sparked by his conversation with Gangnim and Sam-jok-o, Chewy spent most of his journey rehashing the argument with Clint and came to a conclusion. He was no longer the great Chewy Noh, and he needed his friend to know this, but he didn't know how to do that.

That's why he had asked the flower warden for a lucky flower. It was a last ditch effort to go back to the way things were. But there was no going back. Chewy had to face up to who he was now. His life was never going to be easy again.

His power had been everything—solving each little mishap between him and Clint, giving Chewy just the right words to fix any wrong. But now, Chewy couldn't even express this simple idea to his best friend. He couldn't make it clear that he knew his limitations, and it bothered Chewy immensely because if he couldn't get it out, there might be no friendship left.

This worry still bounced around his half conscious brain when he woke early to an empty house. After careful inspection, he came to realize his grandmother hadn't returned at all. She had been out all night.

He went to the kitchen and ate breakfast—a bowl of choco-rings—alone, staring about the room as if his grandmother would suddenly appear. When nothing happened, he got up to take a shower. He hoped this would clear his head.

Afterwards, he stood in front of the bathroom mirror with the morning sun falling in through the small, side window. His shower hadn't helped. A lot had happened in the past two days, and now his time alone was returning. He was afraid what would come of it.

He knew, above all, he had to figure out what to do about Susie. She knew something about Kent's missing body. She had to. He hoped by the time Clint got home from school that afternoon, he would have something to show for all this time alone, like a plan. In the end, he would figure out something completely different.

26
Wrong Assumptions

-Chewy-

The day dragged. Chewy watched TV but found his missing super power still only offered morning dramas and talk shows with all-girl panels. Chewy was dying for a good action movie to lose himself in.

Around lunchtime, he reheated some kimchi soup from the fridge and, again, stared around the empty kitchen. Without his mom, the place felt bigger…and scarier. If his mom didn't come home that night, he wasn't sure he would be able to sleep in his own bed alone again. He shuddered thinking about it.

After eating, he returned to the couch, pushing the remote away. He had enough of TV for one day, which was something he thought he would never say. Besides, he had to come up with something regarding Susie, and it was even more urgent, not just because getting Kent alive and well again was a priority, but also because he wanted to show Clint he could take things seriously.

After an hour of nothing, Chewy decided maybe a change of environment would help, so he shuffled across the door bridge to Clint's room. If anything, he would be able to surprise Clint coming home from school. Instead, it was Chewy who found a surprise waiting for him.

Before he even got the door fully open, his back stiffened, and he held his foot tenuously in the air. In front of him sat Gangnim at Clint's desk, his head down with some papers and a small book that looked like a journal.

"What are you doing here?" Chewy mumbled, stuck in the doorway like a statue.

"Waiting for you," Gangnim said.

At that, he glanced up for a second, and Chewy noticed Gangnim had on a pair of sunglasses. Chewy darted his head around the room. It was midday, and the shades were drawn, covering the room in mild shadows. What were the glasses for?

Chewy lowered his foot back into the bridge. For some reason, he felt this was a good idea. And Gangnim confirmed it.

"Don't worry," Gangnim said, lifting the hand with a pen in it. "Your grandmother's protection ritual prevents me from entering your house. That includes door bridges," he paused for a second, lowering his voice to say, "That is unless you decide to invite me in."

Chewy blinked widely. That was never going to

happen. "So you were just hoping I'd let you on in—to kill me?"

Gangnim dropped his head back, and a giggle popped out. Hearing it, he snapped a hand over his mouth. His large helmet shook as he regained control of himself.

"I can't seem to get rid of them," he said with a cough to insinuate his giggles. "At least, I have the satisfaction of knowing that I'll never have to deal with it again."

Chewy tilted his head. "What do you mean?"

A smile appeared within Gangnim's goatee.

"After you left, I…took care of the flower garden," he said, and his smile dropped to a grimace.

At that moment, a strong odor came to Chewy's nose. After being locked in the school gym while it was on fire, he knew that smell anywhere. Smoke.

"You didn't?" Chewy said, his voice wavering as he thought about the poor flower warden. All he wanted was more people to come and visit. Not this.

"Had to," Gangnim said, lowering his hand slowly to the desk as he mouthed the words, "To the ground."

Then, he looked up to Chewy's large eyes and continued, "Not a single flower left is what I heard. Just means you'd better hold onto the ones you got. They seem to be the last magical flowers in existence."

Chewy felt the blood flow to his face. He couldn't get the flower warden's sad expression out of his head.

"You didn't have to do that!" Chewy blurted out, stepping closer to Clint's room. Images of the burning garden shuffled through his head.

Gangnim stood up abruptly, throwing Clint's chair to the ground.

"You gave me no other option. I wasn't going to have anymore of my special cases pulling ridiculous tricks on me again," he said, turning his body toward Chewy in the door.

Chewy took a step back seeing Gangnim's large, armored form come closer to the closet. Chewy was actually glad Gangnim had those sunglasses on. He didn't think seeing those beady eyes would help his confidence, no less his courage. Before Chewy could utter something back, Gangnim continued.

"Don't think I didn't hear about your little escapade in the underworld too," he said with a sneer. "You come into my domain, making me look like a fool and then leave. I was trying to be courteous, but now—"

Gangnim gritted his teeth, cutting his sentence short. The anger in his voice overflowed, and Chewy visibly shuddered.

Gangnim extracted his sword from its sheath at his side, holding it out for Chewy to see.

"Now, there will be no mercy. There will be no holding back. You've crossed a line Mr. Noh, one that cannot be forgiven."

He then lifted the sword up in the air and plunged it through the top of Clint's desk. He held it there as if stabbing a great beast and then retracted it. Even from the door bridge, Chewy could see the large hole it left, and he gulped nervously.

At that, Gangnim turned to Clint's bedroom door, opening it. Chewy saw a one-way bridge to the underground glow in the doorframe, and Gangnim paused with what looked like a sorrowful expression.

"I had hoped for better from you, Mr. Noh. This will not end nicely." And with one last sneer, he disappeared into the bridge.

As soon as the door closed, Chewy fell to the dark, bottomless ground of the bridge. His legs felt like mud, and his head was swirling—swirling with fear, panic…and something else.

He had the last of the magical flowers in existence. That's what Gangnim said. This echoed through his brain for a second as he recuperated. By the time it stopped, Chewy had figured out how to solve his problems, both with Clint and Susie.

27
I come to a conclusion

-Clint-

Clint dashed up to his bedroom as soon as he got home from school. He knew Chewy was probably bored, if not overly worried. Clint was just praying that Chewy's grandmother had returned with some help. Opening his door, he stopped in his tracks.

Chewy was sitting cross-legged in the door bridge and as Clint scanned his room, he spotted the thrown chair and a gaping hole in his desk.

"What happened?"

Despite his current disappointment with Chewy, at that moment, it faded. Bigger things were going on.

Chewy struggled to get up. Clint had never seen such a serious look on his best friend's face and knew he had something important to say.

"Gangnim was here," Chewy said, nodding toward the desk. To this, Clint's head hung low, his eyes bulging.

His worry started to come back. Going to the underground, he realized that there was little way to change anybody that included his best friend. If it were going to happen, only Chewy himself would be able to do it. Anything Clint did was a waste of energy. Clint's listlessness returned, and his face drooped. Seeing this, Chewy threw his hands up.

"Wait," he said, and Clint raised his head seeing something different in Chewy's eyes. "I've got something to say...but it's kind of hard. Bear with me, please?"

Clint nodded and watched as Chewy pulled a bag out of his pocket. Clint knew what it was immediately. One of the flowers. Before Clint could stop him, Chewy dumped the flower out into his hand.

"There's no reason to freak out," Chewy started. "It's only the truth flower. I need it. I..." His voice trailed off as water gathered in his eyes. Clint didn't move an inch. He had never seen Chewy so vulnerable. And then, Chewy started again.

"I never knew how important my power was," he paused, staring about the room. "You know how last fall, after the fire, I kinda broke that remote control car of yours?"

Clint scrunched up his face. *Kinda?* "You drove it down my stairs! It broke into pieces!"

Chewy wrinkled his mouth in discomfort. "But what happened afterwards?"

Clint glanced at the ceiling to bring back the memory. "You said you hadn't planned on it happening. You thought it would just jump off the first step and land on the floor below."

Clint stared at his best friend, and Chewy nodded, nudging him to continue.

"And then you said I could go over to your house and break anything I wanted. In fact, you said I could break every single thing you owned. You felt that bad about it."

Chewy smiled. "Did it make you feel better?"

Clint nodded, smirking. Chewy did have a way with words. And Clint looked to the truth flower in Chewy's hand. He began to think more was going on here.

"And that's the thing," Chewy said, cutting in on Clint's thoughts. "I was able to do that all the time before, but now, without my power, I have no idea how to fix things when I mess up. I'm learning everything all over again, but—"

He stopped with half-closed eyes. Clint leaned forward, sticking out his head.

"What?"

Chewy lifted his eyes back to Clint's face. "I'm not the Great Chewy Noh anymore."

Chewy's voice was solid and strong, and hearing it, Clint felt like someone had punched him in the stomach. For weeks, he had tried to get Chewy to see this and had given up ever getting through to him. This announcement overwhelmed Clint entirely.

They both stared at each other in silence. It was as if a complete understanding had been reached, and finally, Clint nodded, smiling. Even though Chewy needed the truth flower to get it all out, Clint knew it was Chewy speaking. He chose to do this. His best friend had changed. It just took a little time.

As the feeling wore off, Clint looked to the hole in his desk, and questions began to surface again.

"Why was Gangnim here?"

Chewy took a deep breath and exhaling, explained everything that happened. Clint listened contently, taking a seat on the bottom bunk. It felt like weeks of stress had suddenly disappeared, and being on this side of the conversation was quite enjoyable for Clint. They were working together again. When Chewy finished, Clint couldn't believe what he had heard, especially about the flowers up in the garden.

"Burned them all?" he asked.

Chewy lowered his eyes to say, "yes."

"What are we going to do?" Clint asked, shaking his head. He was happy they had made up, but none of this helped the larger problems they had to deal with. And he heard Chewy cough to grab his attention again.

"With Gangnim's visit, I figured out what we need to do next."

Clint opened his hands, saying, "What?"

"What I just did to you," Chewy said resolutely. "We need to get Susie and the truth flower in the same room. Then we'll find out what she knows."

Being Thursday, they knew there was no way they would have a plan up and ready by the next day, so they postponed any action for the following Monday. The bigger reason being they had no idea what to do. They hoped this extended timeframe would help them, especially in two ways.

First, with luck, Chewy's grandmother would return by then to toss in some advice. But Chewy knew better and didn't withhold from Clint his suspicions that his grandmother might not be back anytime soon. Even with his worries, Chewy was upfront and honest. Clint was happy to see it.

Secondly, without Chewy's smart power, they needed the next best thing to put together a plan, and that was Su Bin.

The next night, Clint slept over at Chewy's like normal. He had done so Thursday night as well but for a completely different reason. The empty house was more than Chewy could handle alone, and Clint had no problem crashing on Chewy's spare bed. The most difficult part was waking up in time to sneak back unnoticed.

That Friday night, however, they went to bed early. They knew they had to be up early in order to synchronize their time to when Su Bin was free. They caught her while studying late into the night, and she all but gladly tagged along, joining them for early bowls of choco-rings at Chewy's kitchen table.

With two bowls in their bellies, Chewy went onto explain what was needed and what they faced.

Susie had to be in the same room as the truth flower along with either Clint or Chewy to get everything to work. The problem was Chewy and Clint had no idea how to do this. By the time they told Su Bin about it, they had come up with many scenarios—the worst involved pushing Susie into the boys' bathroom or trapping her in a dog kennel. They were clearly hopeless, needing a much easier approach, and Su Bin had one.

"Talk to her in class," Su Bin said, her eyes in slits.

Chewy and Clint looked at each other, questioningly.

"How would I get in her class?" Clint asked.

Su Bin's eyes sprang open, and she looked at both of them as if they were idiots.

"Not you," she said, turning her round face to her cousin. "Chewy!"

Chewy's eyes widened. "I don't know if you forgot, but I'm kinda being hunted down by an angry soldier from the underground, not to mention the god of death seems to owe someone my soul."

They both turned to look at Chewy, and he realized that with all the craziness going on, he hadn't even had time himself to digest what had happened in the underground.

"When I went down there," he started, laying his hands flat on the kitchen table as if giving a confession, "I...met the ghost."

Clint and Su Bin's faces turned white with worry.

"Obviously, I got out of there fine, but he said enough to make me believe that not only is death after me, but it seems like he has it out for my grandmother. That's why I freaked out after coming back, and now she's been gone for almost three days."

Su Bin wrinkled her eyebrows in concern before saying, "You think they already got her?"

Chewy shook his head. "If that were true, I have a feeling we'd have heard something by now. I think Yeomra's the kind of guy that likes to gloat. Besides, both of you saw last month how much she likes to do things on her own. She's probably running around somewhere hatching some crazy plan."

With a knowing smile, Clint glared at Chewy as if to say, "sounds familiar."

Chewy perked up his ears, grinning, and put his hands up in front of him. "Hey, that's not me anymore!"

Clint relaxed his face as Su Bin tossed her head between them. Their problems had all but faded away by now. Chewy coughed to settle things down and to regain their focus.

"So as you can see, me going outside is a problem," Chewy said, and Clint nodded with a hum.

Su Bin twisted her lips up, thinking, and then started speaking. "As far as I see it, there's no other way. We've got to get to Susie somehow, and I'd do it myself—we were friends, after all—but I'm not exactly sure how I'd explain coming back from Korea. I think this is our only option."

Chewy looked to Clint. If he wasn't on board, there would be no way of doing it.

Clint lowered his brow, but ultimately nodded.

"There seems to be no other way," he said, turning to Chewy. "It's dangerous, but…if we stick together, I think we can get it done."

Chewy smiled. Having his best friend back on his side was wonderful. He turned to Su Bin.

"So, what do you have in mind?"

Su Bin spent a couple more hours with them, not just to detail the plan, but to have a break as well. Back in Korea, it was almost mid-semester, which meant it was nearing the heavy-testing period. She needed some fun.

After getting the plan squared away, they all collapsed on the couch for an hour or two of TV. But soon, she had to go. She needed sleep after all and was about to pass out in front of them anyway, so they accompanied her to the door bridge and watched her leave.

Clint was a bit somber to see her go. He hadn't seen much of her since the day he died—which was also the day he had told her he 'liked liked' her. He wanted to know what she thought about it, but the opportunity to do so never came up. And it didn't take much for Chewy to see something was bothering his friend, but with everything else to worry about, he decided to set it away for later.

That night, Clint slept in the opposite bed again, and everything was rather peaceful until around three o'clock in the morning when Chewy suddenly sat up in bed.

With all the talk about him going to school, he was dreaming he was back in Mrs. Shapiro's class, answering questions. But something woke him, and he stared around the dark room. He could have sworn he heard something, but, looking over, he only found Clint sleeping soundly.

Chewy turned to his bedroom and closet doors. Being bridges to other places meant anything could come across them, but here, too, everything seemed to be all right. Believing everything was fine, he lowered his head back to his pillow, and that was when finally he smelled it. Smoke.

He sat back up, his backbone rigid. The smell was faint, but it was definitely there. And seeing no fire, he thought of only one thing: Gangnim.

But again, searching the room, he found nothing. After about thirty minutes of waiting, sleep started to set in again, and Chewy felt it might be okay. Besides, hadn't Gangnim said he wasn't allowed to enter Chewy's house while the protection spell was on? The only way to get inside was if someone invited him, and who would be foolish enough to do that?

28
Things get complicated

-Chewy-

The next morning, Chewy shared everything with Clint even though there really wasn't much to share. Chewy wanted nothing to be between them. Despite this, Clint didn't take things so well.

"How do you even know if this protection works?"

They were in Chewy's living room on the couch, and from time to time, Clint watched the walls as if something were hiding in them.

"My grandmother said as much, and so did Gangnim," Chewy said using his calmest voice. Without any skill, he figured this was the best way to approach things. He didn't feel like whipping out the truth flower every time he needed to get something across to Clint.

"Maybe my head was playing tricks with me," Chewy offered to allay Clint's worry. "Either way, I didn't see anything."

Clint shook his head and half-heartedly said,

"You still up for tomorrow?"

Chewy swallowed hard. There was no turning back. It was the only way to get the answers they needed, and he looked to the window behind them to watch the street. Gangnim was out there somewhere. Chewy just hoped he would be able to get one day in the outside world without being hunted down. But, deep down, he knew that would never happen.

Come Monday, they had reviewed their plan thoroughly, and despite being nervous, Chewy somewhat enjoyed the walk to school. He hadn't done so in over a month.

On the way, Clint remembered something.

"Kind of forgot to tell you," he started, "but while you were gone, Miss Wolf, in her own roundabout way, insinuated you weren't coming back because you knew you couldn't cheat anymore."

Chewy's mouth dropped open. The image of Miss Wolf's thin, cold lips and heavy-set eyebrows floated before his face. With all his other worries, he completely forgot he would have to see her again. She was one thing he didn't miss about school.

"Well, hopefully, I won't have to spend too much time with her," he said, even though he knew it was in her classroom that everything was going to happen.

"I just hope this works," Clint mumbled.

But before Chewy could dwell on it more, Clint swung his finger around and said, "You're going to have your hands full."

For a second, Chewy didn't know what he was talking about until he glanced around the bustling schoolyard. The entire place was watching them. In a way, he felt like a celebrity.

They stopped at the back door, and Chewy gave a nod to Mr. Frank.

"Good to see you back Hee-Chu," Mr. Frank said, returning the gesture. Chewy closed his eyes, happy no one besides Clint knew his newer, more girlish name.

Opening his eyes again, Chewy thanked him and turned to Clint.

"I'll see you at lunch," he said and watched his friend hobble inside before he spun around to the field of eyes watching him. After weeks of isolation, he felt he might actually enjoy the attention. On top of it, there was little chance that Gangnim would attack him in such a large crowd.

And he did enjoy it…somewhat. He was able to push off the question of his absence easily—chicken pox—but there was no way around the small line beneath his nose. Everyone gawked at it, causing him to feel self-conscious. When the bell rang, he had never been so relieved. That is until he ran into Becky in the hall.

"You okay?" she asked, wide-eyed in her glasses. He hadn't called her or anything for weeks. She probably felt hurt.

He looked down and mumbled. "Yeah...sick and stuff."

Becky twisted her face up at him. He felt she expected more, but she just walked off, leaving him alone in the hall.

He shook his head. *Girls!*

The rest of the morning went by more smoothly. He received a warm welcome back from Mrs. Shapiro and settled into class. It wasn't until almost lunchtime that he began to notice something unsettling, and as soon as he dropped his lunch tray next to Clint in the cafeteria, Chewy spit out his concern.

"She's been eyeballing me all day," Chewy said, fingering a tater-tot.

Clint looked to him with a questioning stare.

Chewy nodded for emphasis, saying, "You know, Susie."

Clint's eyes glowed with recognition but quickly twisted into their normal worried squint. Chewy tilted his head. *What now?*

Clint took a sip of milk and coughed before speaking up. "The flower's up and ready, but...that's where we might have another problem."

The way Su Bin had devised it, Clint would set up the truth flower high in his classroom so that when Chewy's class went in after lunch for science, the only thing Chewy would have to do is get a seat next to Susie, and soon they would be rolling in answers—or so they thought. Clint's voice picked up again.

"The morning's been a disaster. People have been at each other's throats, blurting out every little secret or thought on their mind. And worse, it's even gotten to Miss Wolf."

Chewy glanced over his shoulder at a very frazzled Miss Wolf. Her face was pale, and her eyes darted around the room as if looking for a wild cat or some other sudden danger. Chewy turned back to Clint with wide eyes.

"We broke Miss Wolf," he said, half-shocked and half-amused.

"This isn't funny," Clint chided. "We barely got anything done above the bickering and fighting. And that just makes me all the more afraid."

Chewy wrinkled his brow.

"What are you talking about?" he asked. "All that proves is our plan is working. Once I get in there after lunch, Susie will be an open book."

Clint set down his fork and stared directly into Chewy's eyes. "That's not it. Anytime someone spoke in class, something unintentional came out. So what's going to happen when you're in there—what unintentional things might come out of your mouth?"

Chewy froze. He hadn't even considered this, and only now did he recall what it was like with Su Bin. There was no way of controlling it, and he realized that this was going to be harder than he had originally thought.

29
A Hint of Me

-Chewy-

This worry stayed with Chewy for the rest of lunch. By the time he got into Miss Wolf's class, he had come to a decision. There was no backing down. He was already here risking his life. Compared to Gangnim, anything he might say in front of Susie didn't look so bad.

And, as usual, the class was a mess with students pushing to get seats. Chewy didn't mind though. He saw Susie in the back corner like always and knew the seat next to her would be open. No one would dare sit there. After all, it was Keith's, the class nose-picker's, desk.

Dropping down in it, Susie glared over at him with large eyes as if to ask, "Are you crazy?" Chewy tossed his shoulders up with confidence. He was done not knowing what was going on. He was here to get answers. But before he could do so, Miss Wolf marched into the class, though her march sounded a little deflated.

"Mr. Noh, I…it is wonderful to see you back," she said. Chewy could tell she was paying extra attention to every word coming out of her mouth. She didn't want to make any more mistakes. "I do hope you'll be leaving—I mean staying with us for a while."

Chewy nodded, smiling genuinely at her discomfort, and he looked to the truth flower hanging above the chalkboard. Clint had done an amazing job. And Miss Wolf continued.

"Today, so far, has been a strange day, so I have some new rules. First, no questions. They've only been trouble. Second, just listen. With luck, we'll get through this class, ah, smoothly."

At that, she turned to the board, and immediately, Chewy twisted his head over to Susie's fearful stare.

All day long Chewy had run through his head what he wanted to say. He even took notes, developing strong, direct questions, but in that moment, with the truth flower staring down at him, all his hard work disappeared.

"You hiding something?"

He cut himself off abruptly, glaring up at the flower. Crap! This was going to be hard.

She squinted at him with her head tilted forward. She had her blond hair tied up behind her which Chewy noted was unusual. She usually liked it flowing down her back.

"Nothing," she said, and a confused look traversed her face. He knew that look well. She hadn't planned on saying those words. The flower was working…but there was something wrong. How could she not be hiding anything?

"I've been in school all day," he pressed on, returning his eyes to Miss Wolf's back. "Haven't seen Kent anywhere. Not that I'm complaining. Did something happen, you know, while I was gone?"

She stuck her lips out but soon found them moving again beyond her control.

"He seems to have run away," she said, her eyes sinking to her mouth before adding, "Or so Tom says."

Ran away? How was she getting away with this? Surely, she knew where his body was. He rummaged through his head for another question, but before he could, she beat him to the punch.

"Since we're talking about it, are you going to finally tell me what exactly it was you were doing the other night?"

"When?" Chewy's mouth spit out, and he began feeling nervous.

"Last Wednesday," she said, and instantly Chewy jumped in to answer her question.

"I was traveling back through a door bridge with a flower that brings people back from the dead."

Chewy paused in horror for a second before realizing maybe that answer wasn't all too bad. Susie confirmed his thinking with a scrunched up face and her follow-up question.

"Are you crazy?"

Luckily, Chewy didn't have to fight this answer back.

"No." And he quickly jumped in to block off any further questions. "How about you then? What were you doing that night?"

"I stood outside your house before going inside," she said as her eyes grew large, and then snapped her hands over her mouth. She began looking around the class in a panic.

"I knew it," Chewy said, snapping his fingers. "So what did you do with Kent's body?"

She shifted her eyes back to him, and even before she spoke, Chewy knew it wasn't going to be what he wanted to hear.

"I didn't do anything with it," she paused, hearing her own words, and then said, "Kent's dead?"

Chewy turned away but not fast enough as his lips slid one word out. "Yes."

Susie's eyes grew larger, and she didn't stop looking at Chewy.

Chewy knew this wasn't good. But it was too late now. With luck, he might be able to leave Susie so turned around that even if she told anyone, it wouldn't make any sense. Before he could say more, Susie's voice chimed in once again.

"What exactly is going on here?"

Chewy lifted an eyebrow.

"I don't know what you're talking about," he

responded, knowing this was true.

"That scar of yours," she said, tipping her nose in its direction. "Today seems to be the first time anyone's seen you with it. But I know that's not right."

He shifted in his seat. What was this? There was no way she could have known about it earlier. After getting it, he hadn't been to school until today. He decided the only way to get to the bottom of it was to be honest. The truth flower no longer mattered to him.

"I got this scar three weeks ago," he said, pointing to his nose. "Why would you say it's not right?"

He could tell by her face that even now she had given up fighting back her answers. They were in this together.

"Over a month ago," she said, her eyebrows sinking. "In the hospital."

A month ago—not possible! Chewy's mind started swirling around. In the hospital—with Becky? And he looked to the seat in front of Susie. Becky wasn't there, but Becky always sat there. He looked around, finally finding her on the other side of the room. There was something else going on here.

"Why's Becky over there?" he whispered out the side of his mouth.

Susie huffed, tossing up her shoulders. "No clue. She sat next to me yesterday. Maybe she didn't want to be around you."

All of it seemed too much for him, and he turned to Susie, looking directly at her.

"When you went into my house last week, what did you see?"

As she stared back at him, he saw her eyes were trembling.

"I saw you—which is why none of this makes any sense." Her voice faded out but he nodded, pushing her on. "It doesn't make any sense because the you I saw last Wednesday had barely any scar at all."

30
More Wrong Assumptions

-Chewy-

The rest of the day Chewy kept replaying his conversation with Susie over and over in his head. None of it made sense, but since the truth flower was present, there was no way she could have been lying. Beyond that, he found it impossible to explain.

Last Wednesday, he had been nowhere near his house or Earth, and he definitely didn't recall seeing her. Every time he hit a dead end with his thinking, only one thing popped up: his grandmother.

Over the past couple of months, he had gotten to know her well—and that included her habit of keeping secrets. He figured she would have learned from the last time when it almost got him and some of his friends killed. Then again, he hadn't yet told her that the ghost from the door bridge wasn't her missing husband, so it seemed keeping secrets kind of ran in the family.

As soon as the end of the day bell rang, Chewy darted into the hall. There was no reason for him to dawdle. He wasn't planning on coming back until all of this was resolved, so there was little to bring home in way of homework.

He saw Clint instantly, and they slipped down the hallway, weaving in and out of other students, making their way to the far end bathrooms. Chewy could already see expectation in Clint's eyes and knew he was going to be disappointed.

He recounted everything Susie had told him, and by the end, Clint seemed just as confused as Chewy was.

"She saw you?" Clint asked.

Chewy nodded, tossing his shoulders up.

"Well, you remember your grandfather's story?" Clint tossed out, to which Chewy batted his eyes.

"Does that mean 'no?'" Clint added, receiving a shrug for an answer. "Do you listen to anybody?" Clint said, straining his voice but continued before Chewy could respond. "The story about Gangnim. Your grandfather said Yeomra was famous for his tricks. You think maybe he's behind it somehow? Gangnim does work for him after all."

Chewy's face uplifted. The story of Samani. He hadn't even thought of it and instantly felt bad for accusing his grandmother of hiding more things from him. What Clint said was much more reasonable.

"But, if that were true," Chewy started, "then

we don't have much to go on. If they're doing all this stuff and somehow got Kent…then we're kind of done, no?"

Clint's face showed he was wondering the same thing, and added, "You may be right, but that doesn't mean we're calling it quits yet. First thing's first, though, we need to get that truth flower out of there before it does anymore damage. I think Miss Wolf was about to have a heart attack."

Chewy pushed out his lips, making his eyes as big as he could get them before saying, "Would that really be so bad?"

The narrow-eyed look Chewy received said it was.

"Alright, alright. Let's go get it," Chewy said reluctantly, pushing into the bathroom.

Chewy made his way over to the back stall and said, "I'll see you in a second."

He swung the door closed and then back open again, revealing the long, dark corridor that connected up with Miss Wolf's classroom.

Most likely she would have locked up by now, so Chewy jogged toward the light at the other end with no worries and peeked out into the empty class.

Within seconds, he had trotted over to the board, staring up at the flower. It was well beyond his reach, and he wondered how Clint had gotten it up there in the first place. He sighed and dragged over Miss Wolf's chair.

Getting the flower in hand, he jumped down and jostled the other bags in his backpack around looking for the empty one. For a second, he wondered how bad it would be to put the farting flower up there for a day.

Before giving it another thought, he heard a deep cough and looked up. Gangnim's grim face stared back at him from across the classroom with a saja on either side. Chewy jumped into a protective stance, shifting his eyes between the two reapers before speaking.

"From what you said before, I thought you weren't a fan of these creatures."

Gangnim raised his head. The sunglasses still sat atop his face.

"I'm not," he said, sneering to show his displeasure for the specters, and then twisted his head around the room. "They're here for another reason. Where is she?"

Chewy lowered his eyebrows. "Who?" he said, eyeing the walls.

"You're grandmother," Gangnim replied gruffly.

Chewy shifted the backpack around in his hand, his free one hovering over the opening. "Your guess is as good as mine."

Gangnim pulled out his sword. "Is this a trick?"

"I wish it were," Chewy said, watching the blade sway in Gangnim's grip. "But my family likes to keep secrets from one another. I don't know where she is."

"Our reports must be wrong. They said she was here."

Chewy wrinkled his forehead. Why would his grandmother be here? Something seemed off.

"As far as I hear, all the tricks are coming from your side," Chewy announced.

Gangnim lowered his sword slightly. "What's that supposed to mean?"

"Some people I've talked to have reported seeing another Chewy. You know anything about that?"

A grin came to Gangnim's face.

"I may know a thing or two about it," he said coyly.

Hearing this, Chewy felt stupid…and angry. All this time, he thought Gangnim was different, was more gentlemanly. In the end, he was just another member of Yeomra's army. Chewy wrapped his fingers around a flower in his backpack.

"You are a fool," Chewy muttered without thinking.

The sly grin on Gangnim's face disappeared, replaced quickly with a vicious sneer. In that second, Chewy knew he had made a mistake.

"My job is to bring you back," Gangnim growled. "And that's what I plan on doing."

To show he meant business, Gangnim swung his sword around in a large swoop cutting the desk beside him in half. Chewy shuddered at the sight of it, watching the desk clatter to the ground. Books and paper spilled out everywhere. And, with that, the sajas unsheathed their own swords.

Holding his hand steady, Chewy flung his head back and forth between the reapers.

"An apology wouldn't help, would it?" Chewy questioned.

Gangnim offered only pale, frozen lips as a reply.

"That's what I thought," Chewy said, opening his stance. "Can't say I gave you a chance."

And Chewy closed his eyes, withdrawing the flower in his hand from the backpack. He stood still for a couple of seconds, his eyes clenched tight. He heard a large vacuum-like whoosh echo throughout the room. For a moment, he thought it had worked until giggling rang out in front of him.

He put the flower back in the bag and opened his eyes. Gangim's sword was lowered, and a smile sat on his face. Beside him, the two sajas were gone.

"A vanishing flower. For that, I have to thank you. I do hate those disgusting things," he said, referring to the sajas, and then tapped a finger to his sunglasses. "Unfortunately for you, I learn from my mistakes."

In that instant, Gangnim lunged, swinging his sword broadly. Chewy dove to the side, hearing the blade cut into the blackboard above his head. He hit the ground hard, grabbing his ribs.

As Gangnim edged closer to the front, Chewy scurried along the wall, putting the filing cabinet and Miss Wolf's desk between them. Before

Gangnim could line up where his target was, Chewy, with his back against the desk, yelled out.

"All of this is because of my grandfather. If I could just get to him, I'd be able to straighten this all out. Please!"

Chewy slowed his breathing to hear better, but no sound came. He flipped his head to either side, afraid Gangnim was already standing over him. Finally, the deep voice popped up.

"You better hold onto those flowers," Gangnim said. "Without them, your future won't be so easy."

Chewy looked over to the door. It was only a matter of feet away. He hoped he would make it, and closed his eyes. *Here goes nothing*, he said to himself, steeling his nerves, and then he jumped out from behind the desk.

At the same moment, Gangnim's sword crashed down through the filing cabinet behind him, missing Chewy by inches.

Chewy slid up to the door and turned around, surveying the room. Despite the danger he was in, he had to smirk thinking of what Miss Wolf was going to do when she found this mess.

He put his hand on the doorknob and stopped, catching Gangnim on the other side of the classroom. They both stared at each other for a second as if trying to read the other's thoughts, and then Gangnim snapped around in anger, slicing another desk in half.

"I'll chase you halfway to Korea if need be," he

said.

Chewy shook his head disappointedly. He had truly believed Gangnim was smarter than this.

"In that case, I gotta go," Chewy said.

Chewy tossed the door open and charged down the bridge back to the bathroom. Before stepping out, he looked back, seeing Gangnim's silhouette in the doorframe. For a moment, Chewy felt sad for the soldier. He was only doing his job, but that feeling didn't last long.

A second later, Gangnim stepped forward, and Chewy's face went flat. Somehow Gangnim had entered the door bridge, and Chewy had no idea how. For all he knew, that was supposed to be impossible.

32
My Plan Begins

-Su Bin-

The alarm broke the morning silence, rocketing Su Bin out of bed. She liked having it across the room so that she wouldn't fall back to sleep. After shutting it off, she stumbled back to bed, sitting hunched over like an old woman. It was too early.

She rubbed her face, wondering how she had made it through the prior day on only an hour or two of sleep. Even now, she felt her body aching for more pillow time, and she shook her head to clean out the fog and regain her thoughts.

Moving over to the closet, she pulled the door open to pick out a dress for the day. She hoped getting dressed would make her feel better, and she flipped her fingers over the stiff clothes. Finally, she yanked out a soft, white one with elaborate frills. She knew she looked extra pure and sweet in it, and this made her wonder what Clint was doing at that second.

The clock told her that by now both Chewy and

Clint should have finished their plan. She hoped they had gotten some useful information out of Susie and were one step closer to finding Kent's body. With that out of the way, they would be able to refocus their efforts on finding Chewy's grandfather. But this wasn't what bothered her.

Ever since the night before, she hadn't stopped thinking of Clint. His face was so pale and worn. She was worried his trip to the underground might have scarred him, and she kicked herself for not somehow asking about his condition before leaving. Above all, she wanted to make sure he knew how she felt. She couldn't help feeling a small pain inside knowing she had only returned his "I like like you" after a death monster had stabbed him. She wanted to make it official.

Still lost in thought, she shuffled over to the mirror in the corner, slipping out of her pajamas, nearly falling once or twice. Her brain was definitely not on yet. Finally, with the dress over her head, she brushed out the wrinkles around the waist, hoping it made her look slimmer. She looked at her reflection, and in that instant, her back stiffened, and her face fell flat with shock. She *had* missed something.

The door to her closet was still open. She spun around looking at the lever to the side of the door and ran through her memory again. Had she hit the switch to open it or not?

She couldn't recall and figured there was only one way to know for sure. She walked back, closed the door, and reopened it slowly. She was right. All she saw in front of her were clothes. It should have been a long corridor to America, to Chewy's bedroom.

She spun around to her bed, her thin eyebrows knit. How could this be? Did this mean something had happened to Chewy?

She stood still as she raced the possibilities through her brain, but none of them made sense except that Chewy was most likely dead. She knew that the bridge's power lay in the spirit of the mu-dang who made it, which only further deepened her concern. However, Su Bin wasn't the kind of girl to jump all in. She had to see to believe, and she ran through the options to get in touch with him.

There was no way she would be able to call. She did the math in her head. Nobody would be at home as it was mid-afternoon in America at the moment, and she knew Clint and Chewy didn't have cellphones. She cringed at the helplessness she felt, and before another second of worry hit her, the phone on her desk buzzed.

The number didn't seem to be one she knew, and she eyed it with worry before snapping it up. If it was going to be the bad news she expected, she wanted it all at once.

"Yes?" she yelled into the phone.

"Is this Su Bin?" a startled but deep voice responded.

She said she was, believing the voice on the

other end sounded familiar.

"I believe you've been looking for me. It's nice to hear your voice again…and so soon too."

In that instant, she knew who it was—Chewy's grandfather!

"Where have you been—I mean, are you alright?"

There was a cough on the other end and his voice jumped in again. "I'm fine. I'm fine. Don't worry. But we need to meet."

Su Bin wanted to say she was thinking the same thing but then, glancing back at the missing door bridge, she said, "Something bad hasn't happened to Chewy, has it?"

Chewy's grandfather immediately responded with an undertone of worry. "Not as far as I know. Why? Do you know something?"

She scrunched up her face, muttering a "no." The whole time she wondered—why now? With all the time they had been searching, he decided to contact them now. It seemed strange. But instead of following through on her instincts, she asked a more immediate question.

"Where are you calling from? My phone doesn't seem to recognize this number."

"That's one reason why I'm calling. I seem to have left my cell phone back at home and haven't been able to retrieve it."

Su Bin lowered herself onto the bed. Things were making less and less sense. "You mean, then, you haven't been home yet?"

"No…been kind of busy. That's why I'm calling. I need to tell you something."

She jumped up from the bed, forgetting the worried feeling that was rising inside. She hoped Chewy was alive because it looked like they were finally going to be able to move forward on getting rid of this curse.

"Let me get a hold of Chewy somehow first and then we'll be right over."

She heard an awkward cough come over the line, and she stopped in her tracks, questioning what was wrong.

"Well, that's the thing," he said hesitantly. "I'm only supposed to talk to you. Nobody else."

She stuck her lips out in thought as she responded. "Why me?"

"Trust me," he said, the confidence returning to his voice. "It'll all make sense…eventually. Now, do you have a pen and paper handy? I'm going to have to give you some directions. Where I'm at is not so easy to find."

32
Gangnim crosses the line

-Chewy-

Chewy jumped into the bathroom and immediately began banging on the door for Clint to open it.

Muttering a frustrated "What?" Clint swung the door wide as Chewy flew through it and turned to his friend with one word. "Gangnim!"

He swallowed again as Clint's face turned white, and added, "Somehow, he's in the door bridge and he's coming this way."

The next couple seconds were a blur as both friends broke from the bathroom, sprinting out the back doors of the school. Chewy tried to keep Clint in front of him until they reached the grass field. They had to do their best to avoid the hundreds of muddy areas, and the last thing they needed now was to slip and fall. Finally, with enough distance between them and the school, they started talking.

"How can he enter the bridge? I mean, I thought

only the people present when a door bridge is made can enter one?" Clint huffed, gyrating like a seal.

"Don't know. The next time I'm stuck in a room with him, I'll make sure to ask," Chewy squeaked, pushing harder on his short legs.

Chewy knew he didn't have it too bad, looking over at Clint's flopping feet. Chewy wasn't even putting his all into it for Clint's sake. He knew too that eventually Clint was going to wear out, and that wasn't an option.

He darted his head back over his shoulder as they cut through the gate, and Chewy caught sight of Gangnim just getting to the grassy edge of the field. In that instant, Chewy knew they had a slight advantage working for them, and he smiled.

Clint saw this and questioned it.

"Gangnim," Chewy said, tossing his head back. "He's slowed down by that ridiculous armor. It must weigh a ton."

Clint wiped some sweat from his forehead as he flipped his head back, too, and then said, "Why don't you just use another flower on him—like the resurrection one?"

Chewy nearly fell over hearing it. He completely forgot that the resurrection flower was still under his bed at home. He was just happy his mom wasn't around to clean. And then he looked to Clint and shook his head.

"Won't work. He's wised up somehow. I tried it in class and it didn't seem to affect him."

Clint wrinkled his face as more sweat poured down. "Didn't affect him?"

"Maybe all you need is a good pair of sunglasses?" Chewy coughed. "Besides, as far as my grandmother's told me you can't kill things like him. I think the best you can do is trap them."

Saying this, Chewy jerked his face and slowed up for a second, feeling the scar under his nose before picking up his pace again. Maybe there was a way out of this after all. He was surprised he hadn't thought of it earlier.

Looking to Clint, he saw his best friend's face had gone red, and his chest heaved more than he had ever seen before. It didn't look good.

"You can't do this for much longer," Chewy muttered.

Clint looked at him with uplifted, worried eyebrows as if to say, "What do you suggest?"

"I know this is not what you wanted," Chewy started, recalling the sad face Clint wore most recently. "I don't want to do this alone, but sometimes we just have to."

Clint hit a thick patch of mud on the sidewalk and skidded, causing Chewy to lunge to his side to catch him before falling over. They quickly righted themselves and began huffing down the sidewalk again as Chewy continued.

"When we turn the corner up here, you're going to dive into Mrs. Johnson's bushes. Make sure you stay low so Gangnim can't see you. Even though I know he's after me, I don't want a repeat of before with Kent. Who knows who they'll kill to get me?"

A tired smile forced its way onto Clint's face. Chewy was happy to see Clint understood. Chewy wasn't trying to do something stupid here. He was hoping to get rid of one of their problems.

"Then what are you going to do?" Clint puffed as they swung around the corner in front of Mrs. Johnson's house.

"Succeed where I failed before," Chewy smiled. "I'm going to trap old Gangnim in a door bridge."

33
How my grandfather met his brother

-Joong Bum-

Unlike the 1944 Summer Olympics staged with POWs from within Germany, the 1952 inter-camp Olympics were never regarded as the triumph of the Olympic spirit over war. Our games were one hundred percent propaganda.

The truth was out there. In every camp, thousands of soldiers suffered from sickness and poor treatment. Among them, a few of us were lucky enough to escape misfortune. We, too, knew these games were a sham thought up by the Chinese and North Koreans to show the world what a beautiful and wonderful heaven communism really was. Never mind the sick and dying.

During the weeks leading up to the games, it was announced that the notorious Camp 6 would host them. Its reputation alone should've scared most away, but I knew for a fact Han Joong was kept there. All the rumors of cruelty in that camp couldn't keep me away. I needed to see family again.

Upon arriving, Jeong and I were off to construct the stands. The communists were diligent in making everything look as good as possible. Even I was amazed at the effort they would go to in order to spread a lie. I had to wonder if they really thought a simple trick like this would fool the world. Maybe, they didn't even know the difference. Who am I to judge?

Eventually, night came and we were exhausted. They instructed us to gather for food, and through the crowd, I saw Han Joong's head pop up and down. It turned out he had heard I was on my way too.

As soon as his arms went around me, I didn't let go and would've cried if I weren't worried about the other soldiers around me seeing it.

He slapped me hard on the back and then pulled me out to see me more properly. "You've lost weight."

"We all have," I said, poking his stomach.

He shrugged and putting his arm across my shoulder, led me to the food.

Jeong tagged along behind us, and through intermittent backward nods, I introduced him to my brother. We all got food and took seats in the corner.

While Han Joong chatted briefly with a person adjacent to us, Jeong leaned over to me with his ridiculously large eyes and chubby cheeks.

"This is him?" he asked.

I had told him much about Han Joong. It was unavoidable, and I might have exaggerated certain aspects.

"I thought he was bigger, at least," he said.

I lowered my eyebrows in a way to tell him to shut up. He didn't take the hint.

"So he's the one married to that pretty girl you told me about?" He scrunched up an eye at Han Joong as if to glean how this short man could get any kind of beautiful girl. I knew better.

"So have you heard?" Han Joong said, turning back to us. We both looked at him with question marks in our eyes.

"I'm on the soccer team. And we are going to crush your camp's team with ease," he said, shifting a thumb behind him. "He's our star player. A Brit!"

We both peeked around Han Joong at the sharp-nosed Englishman he had just spoken to. We didn't see so many Westerners in our camp, and then I realized something.

"You were talking to him?"

Han Joong shrugged a "Yeah, so what?"

"You don't know English," I said, although my voice squeaked it out as a question.

Han Joong smiled.

"I guess I've picked a little up while here," he said, tossing a spoon full of rice into his mouth.

I was surprised at this. Why wouldn't I? But I knew my brother and his skills. Jeong, on the other hand, was overwhelmed by it and stared at Han Joong like some strange god.

I jabbed him in the side, which with all his fat I was shocked he could even feel, but it snapped him out of it, and he leaned again next to my ear.

"Now I understand completely," he said, swallowing hard. "I think even I would marry him if I had a chance."

That's probably another reason why I liked Jeong. We were both horrible idiots at all things.

Before I could respond, there was a loud crash. Everyone turned to the door, and a silence fell upon us. While leaving the food line, an American soldier smacked into one of the North Korean guards. I thought nothing of it, but looking to Han Joong's face, I saw this was not something that would be overlooked so easily. I had never seen such worry on his face before.

The American bent down instantly to pick things up, but then all of a sudden a guard from across the room charged over. There was a grimace on his face and within seconds, this guard drove his knee into the American's jaw, throwing him to the floor.

"Pig!" the guard shouted, stomping over to the sprawled prisoner. As he kicked him once in the side, I noticed a tinge of gray in this ferocious guard's temples, which made him look even more menacing. The man on the floor desperately blocked these attacks but like all of us, he was tired and quite afraid.

The American then tried to get up, and at this point, Han Joong yelled out, "Stay down!" in English. I, of course, had no idea what he said until he told me later. I can only tell you that my brotherly pride grew that day seeing Han Joong help a foreigner.

Not happy with this, the graying guard put his heavy boot on the man's throat, thrusting him back to the ground. He kept pushing on the man's neck until we all heard a sick, choking gurgle. The American couldn't breath.

I stood up without thinking. This wasn't right, and having seen nothing like this before, I felt someone had to do something, but Han Joong put his hand on my shoulder, pushing me back into my seat. Looking over at my brother, I saw him shake his head, and then I realized no one else in the room was reacting. They were just letting all of this happen.

Han Joong gave me a strict stare and said, "Galmae-gi." It meant 'Seagull.'

Afterward, he would explain that this particular guard was famous among the Camp 6 prisoners. And somewhere in the past, he had gotten the nickname. For what reason, I never knew.

It was another minute before a second guard stepped in, pulling on Seagull's shoulder, and as if being snapped out of a trance, he blinked and withdrew his foot.

The American's face had already gone red with eyes rolled upward. As soon as Seagull backed off, two other prisoners dashed forward, lifting the injured off the ground to rush him to the infirmary. Out of rage, Seagull marched off into the night, and slowly people returned to their dinners.

I stared aghast at my brother, and glancing at Jeong, I could see he felt something similar. Han Joong bounced his cold eyes between us before speaking.

"Camp 6," was all he said before lowering his eyes out of shame.

"This happens often—I mean with him?" Jeong asked. His voice came out shaky.

Han Joong looked over his shoulder back to where the scene had taken place.

"Seagull likes to target Americans most often. He considers them the true enemy," he said, and then turned to us. "He doesn't tend to come after us Koreans."

Han Joong started eating again, though reluctantly. But Jeong and I weren't ready to let things go. I had never seen such ridiculous cruelty before. For Jeong, it was something else— something I wouldn't find out till later.

"Are you saying you're alright with this?" I asked.

Han Joong lifted his head again to mine.

"This is the way things are. If you don't accept it…" he turned, looking out a window into the night sky. There wasn't much more he needed to say.

We spent the rest of dinner in silence.

The next morning, the news of the American's death spread quickly. He had passed away in the middle of the night from a crushed esophagus. Till this day, the sounds of that night haunt me.

Part IV: The Underground

34
The Return

-Chewy-

Gangnim's boots clanked loudly with each stomp against the sidewalk, but Clint stayed hidden. He waited just long enough to see him disappear down the block before he got up to follow. No matter what his best friend said, he wasn't going to let him do it alone.

However, despite the small break, his breathing was still all over the place. He was in no condition to run again and took the way home at a brisker trot than an all-out run.

Getting there, he found the front door open. It didn't look good, but entering his house, he realized his mom hadn't even left the basement. He was grateful for that and darted upstairs. What he found surprised him.

His room was completely torn apart. All the papers and books from his desk were thrown to the ground, and he noticed instantly that the incantation was gone from the door. He couldn't help but smile. Chewy had done it!

He went over and opened the closet, finding the long bridge to Chewy's house still there. How could this be? If Chewy's plan worked, the bridge should be gone.

He crossed over, catching further destruction throughout Chewy's room including a split closet door. Chewy's mom was going to kill him when she found out. He called out Chewy's name once or twice, but getting no response, shuffled back to his room.

Sitting down on his bed, Clint's brain began returning to normal, and worry set in. With the door bridge to Korea gone, and his bedroom one still there, Clint only assumed something else had happened. His brain assumed the worst.

Chewy being dead flashed across his mind. Even though there was no body, Clint's eyes began to water. As the pressure began to grow, he heard a slight tap on his closet door.

He stared at it wide-eyed and waited for his tears to fade before whispering a weak "yes."

The door opened, but it wasn't who he expected. Out stepped Chewy's mom, and on closer inspection, he was pretty certain it was Chewy's grandmother. This was further confirmed when she spoke.

"Clint, we haven't got much time, and there's a lot I need to explain to you."

She came closer, lowering herself to look at him face to face as he still sat on the lower bunk.

"Chewy?" he squeaked out.

A smiled came to her face. "You needn't worry. He's fine…and exactly where he needs to be at this moment. But if we want to keep him safe, we've got a lot of work to do."

She stood up again, moving back toward the closet. Clint got to his feet too but then froze as he was bombarded by many inconsistencies. First was her ability to use Chewy's door bridge. And, thinking of how Gangnim jumped in and out of any door bridge he wanted, Clint began to feel maybe they had been lied to somewhere about how they worked.

Chewy's grandmother scoffed at this as she turned back to him.

"No, no. The only reason Chewy can open door bridges is because a bit of my power is in him. In consequence, that kind of makes us the same person," she said, placing a hand on her hip. "And old Gangnim, well, he's a different breed. Gods and other such things can access bridges with ease. Goes with the territory."

She cocked an eyebrow high as if to say, "Is that all?" But Clint's frozen face expressed enough. The bridges were shocking, but only now did he realize he could understand Chewy's grandmother who only spoke Korean.

Seeing this, she waved a hand at him in much the same way as her grandson.

"That's even easier," she huffed, lifting a finger to the flower behind her ear. "When in the room, anyone, despite their language differences, can freely communicate. You could call it an 'interpreter flower,' I guess."

Clint swallowed hard. This meant she had been to the garden too. Chewy's grandmother rolled her eyes.

"You know just because I can read your thoughts, doesn't mean you don't have to talk to me."

Clint lowered his head.

"Sorry," he muttered, "this is a little new to me."

"Understandable." She smirked. "Now, if you're ready. We've got a lot of work to do, if we want to make sure we ever see Chewy alive again."

35
I die

-Chewy-

Leaving Clint back in the bushes, Chewy barely recalled the next couple of blocks. His brain was whirling.

When he did arrive at Clint's house, he slowed to a lull, opening the front door as if it were any other day. He didn't want to raise suspicion.

Chewy knew Mrs. Gill spent most of her time in the basement. He needed her down there with her sewing machine and tiny TV. The last thing he wanted was to put her in danger.

After regaining a modicum of air, he sauntered up the stairs to Clint's room. Immediately, he went to the closet and tore off the incantation from this end of the bridge. It felt like only a day ago he had tried the same thing on the ghost. This time, he was going to do it right.

He sprinted onto the door bridge but stopped midway. Every part of him ached—his body and his mind. He leaned against the wall to rest. There was one more thing he had to do, and soon enough

Gangnim's large shadow appeared in the doorframe.

Despite the heavy armor, Gangnim wasn't heaving at all. This seemed like a normal round of exercise to him, yet Chewy still had not caught his breath. But the sight of Gangnim was all Chewy needed to get his heart going again. Unless invited, Gangnim couldn't come after him, but that's exactly what Chewy needed.

He looked at Gangnim in the doorframe and said, "Come get me!" And then he dove for the other end, getting through the door as fast as possible.

The force of the door closing threw Chewy to the floor. He was more nervous than he thought but quickly righted himself. And just as he was about to tear the incantation off, the door flew open, driving him back to the ground again.

On the floor, he grabbed his head and moaned. His whole body hurt, and he still couldn't get any air, but he noticed Gangnim was about the same. Charging through the door had disorientated his attacker, so Chewy took advantage of this, heading to his closet.

His first attempt had failed. He just hoped the second one would work, and he ripped the incantation off. As he swung the door open to a long, black corridor, he heard a grunt, and glancing over his shoulder, he saw Gangnim back on his feet.

Before Chewy knew it, Gangnim leaned back,

swinging his sword with all his weight. Chewy dropped to the ground without thinking and heard the crack of wood above as the blade pierced the door. Glancing sideways, he saw the long, dark hall to Korea disappear. Only his clothes and unused sports equipment were left in its place.

Chewy marveled at it for a second, realizing there was more than one way to get rid of a door bridge. But he also knew he would never be strong enough to bust one apart.

Luckily, Gangnim's sword was wedged in the wood, so Chewy scrambled under Gangnim's large arms and hit the lever to his bedroom door. The only thing was he didn't know where to go. There weren't anymore door bridges for him to use.

Even though it was a long shot, he knew his only other option was his grandmother if she had returned. He yelled out for her but got no response. The house lay empty. Where was she at a time like this—when he really needed her?

He heard Gangnim tumble to the ground and saw his sword skid across the open door. Gangnim had freed his blade, and Chewy needed to think of something fast.

Tossing his head up and down the hall, Chewy turned to the closet behind him. If anything, he hoped just a plain, old hiding place would be enough. But after opening the closet, he couldn't believe his eyes.

There before him sat another long corridor. He

knew his grandmother had built a bridge there to Korea, but Chewy was nowhere around when it had happened. The fact that it opened up for him was impossible, and yet, here it was. Many peculiar things were happening today, but this moment was not the time to debate it.

He ripped the incantation off the front and launched himself down the hall. Soon Gangnim appeared in the door, and Chewy was beginning to have doubts again, hearing the heavy boots pound after him.

He was much further ahead this time, but already, Chewy's lungs were burning. Still, he pushed with all his might to the other end. He couldn't afford to make a mistake, and getting through on the other side, he spotted Gangnim far down at the other end still.

He smiled, slamming the door. Then with a graceful swipe, he tore the incantation from his end before collapsing to the floor. Within minutes, he was passed out.

Chewy slept for a little more than half an hour before his eyes fluttered open. Even then, he didn't get up immediately. The room kept spinning, but slowly he was able to resituate his head and sat up.

Scooting over to the closet door, he peeked in. It was just his normal closet full of old clothes. No door bridge or Gangnim in sight. Then something troubling dawned on him.

With both the bridge from Su Bin's room to America and this one being gone, that only meant he was stuck. There was no way back to America. Realizing this, he stared blankly at his wall until a small sound from down the hall caught his attention.

Sitting up, he listened closely. There it was again, and he couldn't deny it any longer. He had definitely heard a faint footstep and it was coming from his parents' room.

He got to his feet as quietly as possible. Not knowing what it was, he wanted to be prepared. Having the flowers in his backpack made it difficult to withdraw them when needed, so he put them in his jacket pockets. He didn't want to go through another situation like back in Miss Wolf's class.

He only had time to question what he was doing for a second when he heard a growl from behind. He spun around to find a large, black saja in his open door. It was heaving with its eyes narrowed on Chewy.

"You can't touch me," Chewy yelled at it. "I'm Gangnim's."

It hissed at him, and then said, "That was true. But thanks to you, we don't have to worry about him anymore."

Watching Chewy intently through its eyebrows, the saja took out its sword, and Chewy gulped. It was right. By trapping Gangnim in that bridge, Chewy had just made himself a target for every available saja.

The even stranger thing was he thought the pin his grandmother gave him was supposed to keep him hidden from these creatures, but apparently he was out of luck there too.

Knowing he had nothing else, he thrust a hand out to the seething creature. He was going to have to bluff.

"You know what I've got here," Chewy said, lifting up the backpack in his other hand. It narrowed its eyes, hissing again. "I'll tell you. I have the same flower that took out two of your friends only an hour or so ago. Don't test me."

Chewy shuffled his feet over to the corner. He kept moving backwards until he hit the wall. He had nowhere to go.

"We'll get you eventually. We always do," it snorted, slamming a thick-booted foot down in hopes of putting fear into Chewy. It didn't work. Chewy's nerves were solid by now. He knew what he had to do.

With Gangnim out of the way, the sajas would be relentless from now on, exactly as his grandmother had described them. There was only one thing he could do, and it was at these moments Chewy knew Clint got frustrated with him. He tended to do crazy things, many times just to prove his greatness, but this was different.

"You have someone who doesn't belong to you down there," Chewy snapped, insinuating Kent.

To this, the saja stared at him with distrustful

eyes, taking a step closer.

Chewy breathed deeply, dipping his hand into the empty backpack, and whispered, "Underground, here I come."

At that, he yanked his hand out, gritting his teeth as the saja swung its blade at him. For a second, Chewy thought it was going to hurt. But he was wrong. Dying was kind of like getting a paper cut, and then everything disappeared.

36
My Grandpa begins his tale

-Su Bin-

"Please, take a seat."

Su Bin eyed her toes and then the bare room around her before looking back to Chewy's grandfather's pale face.

"Sorry about that," he said, lowering his head. "The floor should get warm any minute now. I just put in a new bunch of logs."

She smiled and lowered herself to the floor in front of a small table about a foot off the ground. It was a customary table brought out when guests came, and Su Bin wondered for a moment what Clint would do if forced to cross his metal legs near this thing.

"Did you have a hard time finding the place?" he asked as he began pouring some hot wheat tea into a tiny porcelain cup in front of her.

She shook her head, holding the cup with two hands.

"Your directions were pretty exact." She hesitated and then said, "I've never really been out in the country before."

To this, he smiled, drawing thick lines around his eyes.

"Yes, I would believe that is quite common for young people today." He paused as if musing over something and then with a shake of his head, continued, "It's wonderful to finally meet you face to face. Though to be honest, I expected someone a little bit…"

"Prettier," she spit out, uplifting the middle of her eyebrows.

He batted his eyes, startled. "Not at all. I was going to say taller. I thought Chewy's shortness came from his mother's side of the family."

Su Bin smirked, her eyes disappearing into two smiley lines.

"And now I see where he gets those eyes from," he said, looking upon her warmly, and then continued in a wistful tone, "Besides that, you remind me a lot of Chewy's grandmother."

She lowered her eyes. She knew he was just being nice to her. It was the way Koreans were. Upon first meeting almost anyone, they complimented the other's appearance.

"I don't think so," Su Bin murmured. "I heard she was quite beautiful."

"Oh she was! So many men loved her, and the funny thing was she never paid attention to any of them." He paused, taking a sip. "I'm sure you know what that's like."

She jerked her head up at him in surprise and he

began to chuckle.

"Don't think you can fool me," he continued. "I may not speak English, but when you called me last month, I heard everything, including your giggles for that American friend of Chewy's. I may be old, but I know when a girl is flirting."

Su Bin's face grew red, and for a second her eyes were actually quite large. But before she could respond, he had moved on.

"I remember Sae-rim was the same—that's Chewy's grandmother—though she only ever laughed for Han Joong. It drove me wild. What I would've given to have any girl laugh like that for me."

His eyes grew misty, and Su Bin decided to move the conversation on.

"You know something then…that can help?" Her voice was filled with worry. She still had no idea whether Chewy was okay or not, and she didn't know if all of this was maybe just a little too late.

He nodded to her question, sticking out his lips in thought. "You know, Han Joong was the handsome one."

Su Bin snapped her head up.

"Chewy said you guys looked almost identical, that's how you were able to—" She clapped her hands over her mouth. The fact that he wasn't the real husband of Chewy's grandmother was supposed to be a secret.

He smiled warmly.

"It's okay," he started weakly. "I was going to tell you about it now anyways."

At that moment, a concern popped into her head.

"About that," she hummed, "why are you telling me? I mean, why not wait for Chewy?"

For a second, his face went flat, and a worried look traversed his eyes. Then he said, "That I can't say. There is a reason why, but it'll take time to figure out. Until then, let's just say I'm telling you because you need to know."

She had no idea what to think about this and drew her hands around the weak tea for warmth. In the end, she figured it didn't matter as long as they got the information they needed to end the curse.

"So…you guys didn't look the same?" she said, hoping to get things back on track.

"No, we did—very much so. It was only if you put us next to each other that you'd see a slight difference." He paused, lifting his eyes in thought as if drawing up an old memory. "But it was when Han Joong talked that we looked like opposites. Everyone could see it in an instant. He was the amazing one."

Chewy's grandfather lowered his head before continuing.

"If it weren't for the war, I'm sure he'd have done some astounding things. A politician maybe. Or company owner. He had potential. I was never going to be like that. I was bad at sports, talking, and even school. This, of course, was before parents put so much emphasis on studying. Still, I was no scholar."

He smirked at the thought of it and added, "That's probably why I was so worried for Chewy when he was younger, you know, not being good at school and all. I was able to easily relate. His mother didn't have those problems."

Su Bin coughed politely to break in, and said, "I don't know if you've heard, but…Chewy's kind of lost his power. He's back to the way he was before."

She studied his face for a semblance of pain, but nothing showed. When asked later, she would swear it looked like he already knew this information. But before she could say more, he jumped in, acting as if he hadn't heard a word she said.

"As for me, my destiny was to take over this farm. I was going to be a rice farmer like my dad and his dad before him. And it would have happened. But then one day, the North crossed the border, declaring war on us. And with it, my life, as well as my country, changed forever."

37
My Grandma's Plan

-Clint-

The energy began to build in the room, and Clint just watched on as Chewy's grandmother in full Korean ware spun around in front of his bedroom door. She wasn't the only thing that was spinning. Clint could barely keep his thoughts steady. According to her, he had a lot to do.

After coming across the door bridge, Chewy's grandmother explained everything to Clint. After all, he was an important part. She had said so from the beginning.

"That first day—the day when Kent was killed, as soon as I walked into the house, I saw something was off," she said in a quickened tone from her perch on Clint's desk chair.

She was crouched over to look at him in the face. Clint just stared. What was there to say? And she continued, not noticing if he was following or not.

"Now you have to understand, Yeomra can

never be trusted, and that's what has made this all the more difficult. Every step of the way, I doubted myself and what I saw, but eventually, it made sense." She paused for effect before saying, "My future self had figured a way to save Chewy…only I didn't know how at that moment."

Clint's face scrunched up. "Your future self?"

Chewy's grandmother shuffled around in the chair. Lines of frustration sat on her forehead.

"It doesn't matter if this makes no sense now. One day, it will, and you are extremely important to making sure this plan works."

He lifted his eyebrows to see her more clearly. He was happy the whole Noh family was finally including him in their plans. He wouldn't feel this way for long.

"What do I have to do?"

She gritted her teeth, sighing.

"I'm not a hundred percent on that part," she said and then raised a finger to stop his objection. "But I can tell you what we need to do next. First, I'm going to build a bridge from your bedroom to Chewy's."

Clint wrinkled up his brow again. That didn't make sense.

"We already have one," he stated matter-of-factly, pointing to the closet she had just come from.

She shook her head. This didn't seem easy for her. Despite the flower helping with translation, Clint wondered if she just wasn't used to all this

English.

"No, no, no. We're going to make a bridge to his Korean bedroom," she said, and stared at Clint for a second as if weighing something important in her head before saying, "That way we can retrieve his body."

Hearing this, Clint nearly fell off the bed. Luckily, she was fast enough to catch his arm to keep him upright.

"He's dead?" Clint blurted out, his eyes popping from his head.

"For the most part…yes," she muttered.

Clint pulled himself back on to his bed. "In what way isn't he dead?"

She snapped one eye shut in thought as she chose her words. "Well…his soul's not dead, and with luck—which I'm pretty sure we have—he'll get out of there alive."

Clint sighed, dropping his shoulders for a second before another concern surfaced in his brain. "Then why do we need this bridge?"

She sat back to look at him better. "Besides having no other way back to America, it may take him some time to return to his body. If we aren't careful, there may be no body to come back to."

Clint tossed his head around. How come everything she said didn't make sense? He knew this wasn't a Korean thing. Chewy spoke unbelievably clear and straightforward.

"Are you saying someone else might steal his body like Kent's?" he asked.

She stuck out her lips searching for a way to explain. "First of all, Kent's body is fine—"

Clint again rocketed forward, spitting out a "what?" before settling down. "You mean you've known where Kent's body has been this whole time?"

She glared at him.

"I can answer that question with a definite 'No, I did not.' But," she said, raising a finger, "I know perfectly well that his body is safe for him to return to, which is exactly what we have to do for Chewy."

She cleared her throat, keeping a finger up to hold Clint off and continued, "The human body begins decomposing within seconds of death. So we need to get his body to a safe place as soon as possible."

Finally, she dropped her finger and Clint jumped in instantly. "And where would that be?"

She chuckled for a second to herself, looking up to the ceiling before answering.

"I forgot, you don't know all this stuff like I do," she said, lowering her eyes back on him. "Door bridges, in their own way, manipulate time. They are…beyond time, so to speak, like pockets of nowhere. For that reason, nothing technically ages in them."

Clint perked his head up. "So if I stayed in one, I'd never get older?"

She nodded to his question and shrugged as if this idea was perfectly natural. Then she said, "So you can see why we need to get Chewy in one. His cells will stop falling apart then."

Clint stared off into the distance, confused. "But wasn't Kent's body lying out for days?"

"Not really," she said, hesitantly. "I moved it as soon as Chewy went to the upper realms. I knew it would start decaying so I tossed it into an old bridge of mine for safekeeping. And then…"

Clint looked deadpan at Chewy's grandmother. He was beginning to feel like he was talking to Chewy. He now knew why they fought so much. They were identical.

"And then…what?" he asked.

"That's part of what you'll find out in time," she said, shifting in her chair. "Now stop asking questions. I need you to do this while I'm busy finishing my end of the plan. Once this is over, I'll explain everything in much greater detail, okay?"

It was the best he was going to get, so he nodded. A satisfied look appeared on her face, and Chewy's grandmother stood from the chair with an air of relief and began the bridge building ritual.

Clint watched and felt the room grow with energy. None of it made sense, and he couldn't get his head around the fact that Chewy was actually dead. Maybe he would be alive again soon, but what really bothered him was that once the bridge was completed, he was supposed to cross it and retrieve his best friend's body. He tried steeling his nerves, but every time he looked down, his hands were shaking.

Suddenly, with a clap, the whole ritual ended, and he lifted his head to Chewy's grandmother. She put a hand to her chest and glanced over at him. "We don't have much time."

She swung the door open, pointing down the long corridor. He swallowed hard and got up from the bottom bunk. As he passed her, he swore he smelled smoke but dismissed it, stepping onto the cold, black of the bridge.

Looking around into the darkness, he couldn't help but shiver, recalling her words. *Door bridges are beyond time. Pockets of nowhere.* As if their eternal darkness wasn't freaky enough.

Halfway through, he twisted his head back and saw nothing but his empty room. Chewy's grandmother was gone. Clint desperately wanted to understand everything, but he knew there was little time for that now.

Getting to the other side, he eased the door open with a squeak, his eyes half-shut. He fully expected to see a saja hanging over Chewy's dead body, its cape blowing in the wind. But there was nothing.

He stepped into the room to survey his surroundings. The way everything was shifted he knew something had happened here, and then he spotted Chewy's body. He tiptoed over, believing at any moment it would sit up and start talking. He didn't look dead at all.

Standing above his best friend, Clint felt a chill

run through his body. Chewy was dead, and as he grabbed Chewy's still semi-loose arms, he began dragging him to the bridge. He hoped Chewy wouldn't be dead for too long.

38
Death's Plan Falls Into Place

-Chewy-

The next couple of minutes after the saja's sword pierced through Chewy's chest, he felt turned around. It was like those moments when the power goes out, and one suddenly strives to realize what has happened. Darkness is something no one expects, and Chewy had no idea where he was.

But, eventually his mind refocused, and he found himself following a small path in the darkness. He recognized it immediately. Another path swung around it, crossing it from time to time. It was the road to Death.

Glancing over his shoulder, Chewy saw the saja, and his eyes locked for a second with its grim stare. If all the tales were right, these creatures led souls to the underworld and were almost impossible to escape from. But the thought of escaping never crossed Chewy's mind.

In a matter of minutes, a low moaning came

from the fog ahead. Chewy slowed down hearing it, but the saja pushed him on. Getting closer to the sound, Chewy saw a thick river of black twisting and turning upon itself. But, soon, he realized this wasn't water. These were the gaekgwis.

From what he remembered from Gangnim's tale, gaekgwis were the lost souls forced to roam forever just outside the underground. They were ghosts who had become trapped between the living and the dead. This was due to their improper burials or their lives being taken while away from home, and they were now cursed to be ghosts forever. They were collectively pitied but just as much feared. For everyone knew these ghosts would do anything to move on.

The saja took a step forward and stuck his arm out in a sign of caution. Inching closer, Chewy felt overwhelmed by not only the gaekgwis' incessant moaning, but also by the long, black faces each specter wore. None of them had eyes or mouths. In their places were large, gaping holes.

The saja drew its sword, bringing Chewy into the moving crowd. At first, the black spirits bent around them, but soon it was as if all the gaekgwis had come to a realization. There was something special here, and they all wanted to take part. In an instant, one grabbed a hold of Chewy's wrist. He looked to the saja in front, but noticed the gaekgwis had already sprung between them. Another one looped around Chewy's ankle while a third one slid along his belly. Their touch felt like snakes, but he was too scared to scream.

Then one of the tar-like ghosts yelled. "He's got it with him!"

And like a large tsunami, the other gaekgwis tumbled over toward him. Chewy no longer saw any part of the saja, and his heart was pounding so fast it sounded like drum beats in a crazy parade.

Dark hands wrapped around his head, and for a moment, Chewy caught a glimpse of the saja swinging its sword wildly, slicing these black specters in two. But it didn't last long as another tidal wave of them came crashing down, and in that second, Chewy felt he had maybe made a mistake.

The March darkness closed around Susie, causing her to shiver. It moved in so slowly that it was hard to tell when day actually became night. She pulled her hood up, feeling a smattering of rain on her face. Despite this, she wasn't going to move from her post in front of Chewy's house.

He had told her Kent was dead. There was no way he could know something like that. It was impossible, unless…

She shook her head. No. Not even Chewy would go that far. He was rude. There was no doubt about that. But as much as she hated him, he had helped Becky with her math, and he did have that disabled boy, Clint, as a best friend. All of this made it harder for Susie to know what she had to do.

But wasn't this exactly what she always saw on late night TV, on those shows about murderers and serial killers? It was always the kind-hearted, seemingly normal ones that turned into monsters. But again, this didn't make sense.

She kept coming back again to their conversation in science class, and what seemed particularly unsettling was that he didn't even realize what she was talking about. In fact, he was just as surprised as she was. And this only disturbed her more.

She took out her cellphone, eyeing the number pad. She bent over slightly to protect the screen from the occasional drops and stared deeply into it. This was a big step, and she didn't know if it was the right one.

She brought her head back up to Chewy's yellow house. He hadn't come home from school. She knew because she came straight here, and she never saw him. This only meant two things. Either knowing he might get caught, he ran away; or he was out covering his tracks.

She squeezed her eyes, hoping something would come up to give her a push in one direction or the other. But reviewing it again, she came to one conclusion. If Chewy didn't know about the other places and things he had done, it meant Chewy had a brain problem. Maybe, he wasn't even aware of the horrible things he did to others. This made it all the scarier for Susie, and with her thumb, she punched the three numbers into the phone.

Afterwards, she placed the earpiece to her head, hearing the drone of it ringing. Finally, the other end picked up.

"Emergency 911. How may we be of assistance?"

Susie took a deep breath and jumped in.

"I'd like to report a dead body.

39
How my grandfather's life came to an end

-Joong Bum-

The games proceeded, and I was happy to watch Han Joong out on the field for one or two of his matches. In the end, Camp 1 got first place, and I was able to gloat, as my camp—Camp 5—took second.

"I'm sure you were a big asset to your team, watching from the stands," Han Joong ragged me while rubbing my head.

He then put his arm around me as we stood against the back fence to catch some of a soon-ending softball game.

I had to admit it. Our captors had done well. It looked professional enough, and the POWs enjoyed themselves, reveling in hits and outs like they were back in their home countries.

"Where's your sidekick?" Han Joong asked, insinuating Jeong with a jab of his elbow.

I hadn't seen him all morning. After everyone woke up, his bed lay empty. I thought nothing of it, believing he ran ahead for breakfast or to finish his duties to make it to another game of football. We had never seen such a sport before and there was something about large guys slamming into each other that particularly fit Jeong. Maybe because of his size, he figured it was a sport he wouldn't be half bad at.

"No idea," I said, feeling Han Joong's arm tighten around my shoulders. I looked up at him, and he nodded in the direction behind the stands.

We walked together, hearing the subtle din of applause fade behind us. To the left, another match was going on, but it was hard to see what it was. With some time alone, we strolled, kicking rocks along our path between the bunks and the playing fields.

A sentimental shine took to his eyes. I could tell he was thinking about something serious, something about home.

"How is it?" he asked.

I shrugged. There really wasn't much to say, and besides, I wasn't about to tell my big brother how, with him gone, I felt like I had been living in his shadow. Brother's didn't say those kind of things to each other.

"Mom treating our little Sae-rim okay?" he asked.

His eyes glowed as if made of glass, and I couldn't help but cringe a bit. I'm not sure why I did, but maybe it was because I had no one at home waiting for me.

"In the beginning," I said, rubbing my chin as if it were impossible to describe, "Sae-rim took it hard. Mom worked her like a horse. Says you need a strong woman...like herself."

He laughed loudly. "The last thing I need is another mother nagging me wherever I go."

I laughed too, knowing well how sharp our mother's tongue got. I knew even better how sharp Sae-rim's was. My childhood was decorated with shouting matches between her and me.

"But Mom got her to cook well."

His eyes bugged out.

"Impossible," he said, waving it away.

I put my right hand up to prove I was telling the truth.

"Eventually...even Gwan Sae-rim can change, I guess," I mumbled.

He smirked. "You remember how she always made those potatoes for us, don't you? Dumping them in the fire the way—as she would say—her grandma taught her."

I nodded, thinking about the fire in our backyard as he continued.

"All she had to do was make sure they weren't in the flame for too long, yet every single time, her potatoes tasted a little burnt," he said, scrunching up his face in displeasure.

"Remember when we'd bring it up to her?" I mentioned, waving some of the floating dust away from my face. The sun was lowering over our shoulders drawing large shadows off the one-stories around us.

He grinned again at my comment. "She would deny it forever. That's just good flavor, she'd say. Couldn't even admit they were burnt...not even a little bit," he said, shaking his head. "So stubborn...but the girl is cute."

Saying this, he turned his head to mine as if knowing my inner thoughts, my deepest secrets. Han Joong always thought he was so sly, but I cut him off.

"Not anymore," I howled, smirking.

He looked at me with a questioningly glare, and I explained.

"Mom's already worked her so hard, all the baby fat's gone from her arms and legs. She's about as skinny as me now," I said, sticking an arm out.

He put on an overly fake frown. None of this mattered to him.

"Too bad," he said. "At least now, both of you will look the same—after all that hassling you gave each other as kids."

He winked at me, and I pushed him away.

Then, at that moment, we heard a voice pierce the dimming sky. By now the match was far behind us so the air had grown quiet. We shuffled over to the wall of one of the barracks, holding close to it. The last thing we wanted was to get caught out, wandering around.

Han Joong peeked around the corner and waved me to run to the shadow of the adjacent building. I did so, and soon he joined me. Both of us were breathing heavily more out of fear than exhaustion. Then we heard it again.

"…so smart…"

Han Joong snapped his head toward me. We both knew whose voice it was. Seagull.

I pointed behind us with my thumb. Getting closer didn't seem like a good idea, but Han Joong had to see. The rest of my life I wish we had just turned and left. Maybe things would've been different. Maybe I wouldn't be telling this story today.

We got down low and peeked around the corner, catching the open yard where we gathered on good days. In the middle, we saw Seagull with a cloud of dust at his feet. He was kicking something.

"We're the same," he screamed with spit flying. His mouth opened like a braying donkey. "And you go and help them, protect them!"

Seagull began pacing. He looked certain that his prey was immobilized. Besides, his red face and quickened breath showed he was tired. He needed a break, and during that time the dust settled enough for us to see the man on the ground with his stomach arched upwards. It wasn't hard to distinguish his features. It was Jeong. I drew a hand to my mouth.

"I…can't feel my legs," he murmured.

I shivered hearing this. I had heard about the torture some POWs endured. One common practice was the stick torture. The way it worked was they'd put the prisoner on his knees, but just below the kneecap would be a stick. Essentially, this stick would end up cutting off all blood to the prisoner's calves. If left there long enough, they'd never be able to walk again.

Jeong shifted in pain. I knew that was a good thing. It meant the nerves were still functioning in his lower legs, but it didn't help the situation as it drew Seagull's attention back on him.

"You're going to be my message to the rest of them—to show them what happens when you put foreigners above our own kind."

Seagull spit on him and drew his head back sharply as if disgusted.

I could see Jeong had no energy left in him. There were tears streaming from his large eyes. He turned for a second and the necklace his mother had given shifted around his fat neck. Something inside of me ached.

Seagull turned his small head down toward Jeong. His eyes were small and black and lacked all compassion imaginable.

"You had your chance before," he said, lifting his boot off the ground, and placed it squarely on Jeong's neck. "You should've stayed with us—stayed with the winning North."

Seagull raised his chin to look down at Jeong in pride. His knee was still high enough not to choke him.

I felt Han Joong's hand on my shoulder. It was

as if he was saying, "There's nothing we can do. It's too late."

And then Seagull lowered his heel and said, "Those who turn their backs on us, disappear."

40
A Reunion

-Chewy-

Slowly, Chewy's eyes began to focus. The darkness made it hard to see but he knew, for some reason, the gaekgwis had let him go. He stretched and found himself by another stone pillar like before.

He backed up next to it, looking wildly into the darkness. The moaning still rang out in the distance, and he swore he saw something moving. Then, finally, it breached the curtain of black, coming into view.

It was one, sole gaekgwi dragging itself closer. Its arms hung low, and on its face, the gaping holes of the eyes and mouth startled Chewy. Even the old ghost's red eyes were better than this.

Despite it being alone, Chewy did not relax. He didn't really understand these creatures at all. He only knew the mythical tales he read in scary comic books. But this was real!

As it neared him, he saw its inky skin pull tight

over its shape as if something were hidden inside, and slowly, a human face appeared. With it, a shock of black hair careened off the top, and it began to look more and more human. Finally, the wisp of black surrounding it sank away like a magician's trick cloak, revealing a human form in torn clothes. It looked Korean.

"You're the boy, aren't you?" it said, speaking with a North Korean accent.

Chewy shivered hearing it. He had only heard such accents on TV or in movies.

"I don't know what you mean," he responded.

The ghost put up its hands as if approaching a wild tiger, and said, "I mean no harm. It got out of control back there."

It shifted its head to the darkness, tossing a thumb toward the fog and then looked back to Chewy before continuing, "You have to be careful. Gaekgwis will do anything to get out of this place. Being dead or alive is a much better option."

Chewy didn't budge or take his eyes off the thing. It looked so human now that he couldn't believe it had been that inky creature before like the others.

"You did this?" Chewy asked, referring to pulling him out of the stampede.

It nodded. "I couldn't help it. You look just like someone I knew."

Chewy looked down. He wasn't sure if that was a good thing or not, but at least this ghost had feet.

It was much scarier when they didn't, floating around in the air and all.

"Who do I look like?" Chewy squeaked out.

The ghost took a seat but kept its hands up to show there was no harm, and then said, "Two brothers, actually. We were in the war together."

Chewy tilted his head. Brothers?

"You mean Han Joong and Joong Bum?"

A smile came to its face.

"Yes," it said, bowing slightly. "Everyone then called me Jeong."

Chewy bowed back. He wasn't about to disrespect a ghost.

"You look just like them," it continued, and then pointed to Chewy's face. "Except in the eyes."

"My dad's side," Chewy explained and sighed. He was happy to find at least one person, alive or dead, that didn't hate his grandfather.

"How are they, then?" it asked.

Chewy could see the ghost's face light up. Getting news from the world above must be rare, especially about people it knew. And then Chewy realized something. The ghost had asked about both of them.

"They?" Chewy asked, screwing up his face. "Are you saying Han Joong's not down here?"

The ghost's face went flat.

"Of course not," he said solemnly. "I've been waiting. None of your family has gotten remotely close to the underground. Otherwise, I would've known."

It smiled, waving its hands to calm Chewy, and slid a little closer.

"Even your grandmother hasn't made it down here yet." It winked at Chewy. "You should've heard the things they had to say about her."

Chewy smiled back. For a ghost, he seemed quite friendly, and Chewy leaned over to appear more open.

"She should be down here," Chewy said. "But became a mu-dang spirit instead. Possessed my mom. A little bit of me too."

It pushed its chin out as if to say, "Is that right?" Then it leaned over closer as well, sliding ever so slightly forward.

"So tell me," it started, "since you believed Han Joong was actually down here, does that mean old Joong Bum ended up with that pretty, little grandmother of yours? I figured Han Joong would take her back eventually."

Chewy looked down. Only now as he thought about it did he realize how hard it was to talk about. Life would've been better had his grandparents stayed together.

"Not really," Chewy mumbled.

The ghost pulled itself up beside the pillar next to Chewy. Then while humming its sympathy, it dropped its arm across Chewy's shoulder and patted Chewy's knee with the other hand.

"It's okay. Everything will be okay soon," it said.

Chewy nodded for a second but then stopped. Why would everything be fine soon? Before he could ask, the arm on his shoulder slipped around his neck. Chewy grabbed it, but it was too late, already he found it hard to speak.

"Shhh...don't fight it," it whispered.

Chewy wrestled back against the ghost's grip but couldn't move anywhere. Its other hand was already holding him down. It was remarkably strong.

Chewy looked over and noticed its eyes had disappeared into an inky black again, and it hissed at him before speaking. "Where is it?"

Chewy's eyes felt strained, and he coughed out a "What?"

"The flower," it snapped.

The flower? Chewy tried shaking his head. He had many. Which one was this thing talking about?

It screamed out. "I know its here, you fool. Why do you think the other gaekgwis went crazy? It's our only way out of here, and I'll rip you apart to get it!"

Large fingernails grew on its hand, and slowly the ghost lowered it toward Chewy's stomach.

"Just give it to me and I'll let you go."

Before Chewy could answer, he saw a figure move quickly through the fog. It was the saja with its sword drawn, and it dropped its blade across the ghost's arm. Its hand toppled to the ground, turning back into black goo.

Chewy then heard the ghost scream, and he slid away as the saja drew its sword back and chopped off the creature's head.

Chewy lay heaving on the ground, staring at the black mess that was the ghost. Then he looked up to the saja's emotionless face.

"Let's go," it said and started moving into the darkness. Chewy wasted no time following after it. Having to choose between a saja and a gaekgwi, Chewy figured the saja was clearly the better choice.

The dark soldier led Chewy through the underground's gates. This time few gaekgwis stood in their way. As they passed, Chewy saw the ones the saja had chopped in half earlier were slowly putting themselves back together. It reminded him of movies he used to watch, but soon he forgot it all looking over the vast darkness of the underground.

There were mountains and pillars everywhere. In the distance, small huts broke from low hanging clouds. He wanted to pause to get a better look but the saja pushed him forward, and soon it all disappeared into mist again.

The only thing Chewy knew was the incline of the path before him felt sharp and he had to lean backwards as he went, going deeper and deeper.

Finally, he saw a sort of cage ahead, and getting closer, the figure inside it began to grow. Chewy realized he knew who it was.

Kent.

41
The Moment

-Chewy's Grandmother-

They had told the mu-dang that a body had been reported, but upon searching the house, the two officers, one short and the other tall, found nothing even remotely suspicious—no less a missing boy's corpse. Stepping outside with her onto the stoop, the two men nodded, apologizing for the inconvenience, and turned down the walk.

The mu-dang just stood there, watching them go before slipping on a pair of sunglasses as she reentered the house. Someone was waiting for her.

She returned to the kitchen, bustling over a steaming kettle of tea to the table. Otherwise, she had a full spread prepared: cake, some rolls, and popped-rice—a Korean favorite for munching.

After situating all of it, she put her hands on her hips to marvel at her work and then looked at the clock. *Him and his drama*, she thought.

She started whistling as she turned to her stove and let out a strained cough. With neither working, she just spit it out.

"They're gone," she said, leaning over to the hallway.

The floor creaked from Chewy's room, followed by slow footfalls down the hall. And the whistling resumed, this time by the man, coming to her kitchen. He stopped curtly at its border.

The mu-dang didn't even turn around. Dignifying Yeomra and his antics only seemed to encourage them. This did not stop him from smiling though.

"Come now, just games and all that kind of thing," he said, twirling a gloved finger.

"Might as well sit down," she said. "You've come this far."

She was insinuating his little ruse with the police.

"Well, you did seal this place up pretty well," he said with an undertone of blame.

She snorted, waving a hand at him.

He hummed in agreement and slid into the chair on the opposite side of the table. Immediately, he looped an empty teacup in his pinky finger, hanging it dangerously like a child would.

"Does smell good though," he said out of the side of his mouth before straightening himself up. "So when'd you know?"

"Just after they came in. You were clearly riding on the taller officer. Couldn't get a clean thought out of him," she said. "But it was going to happen eventually, no? Your 'men' having been around my house far too much."

She meant his sajas to which he scoffed.

"They draw such attention to themselves," he said, finally bringing the cup down to its saucer. "Do you mind?"

She tossed a hand up over her shoulder, muttering a "help yourself." He dove in immediately, breathing in the steam as it came off the tea in his cup.

Then he lifted his head as if nothing important was going on at all and raised one closed hand in the air.

"We almost lost one of them there when looking under the bed," he said, opening his hand to reveal a pink flower. "Good thing I was there to scoop it up."

She turned around catching sight of the resurrection flower in his hand, and he stuck out his lips at her sunglasses.

"Shame. Thought I'd catch you off guard," he said, flicking his tongue at her guile.

"I know what to expect from you," she said, tapping the sunglasses.

He showed a wide, thin-lipped smile to her roundabout compliment. "Your type never disappoints. Why anyone would make laws against your kind is beyond me—and I mean that in the best possible way."

He lifted the cup up and nudged it in her direction as praise. She wiped her hands on the apron, took a seat, and then noticed his finger pointing to the flower behind her ear. She had forgotten to take it out after the police left.

As she removed it, she watched him gingerly sip the tea. She was happy to have the sunglasses. Yeomra had his yellow eyes as protection from the flowers, and she wanted to be on level ground with him. And a smile came to her face seeing him enjoy his tea.

Setting the cup down, he slipped the resurrection flower into an inside jacket pocket, tapping it for safekeeping.

"Everything's almost done…my part anyways," he picked up, flicking a wrist. "As far as my reports say, Chewy's down where he belongs as we speak. Looks like, in the end, you lost."

The mu-dang nodded solemnly and picked up her tea. She signaled a "Cheers!" with it and took a sip. She figured it was only fair that she dive into the tea too. She wasn't a trickster after all.

"So why are you here now? You've got what you want."

He tilted his head, smirking.

"Yes, but we gods sometimes find ourselves in peculiar situations," he said and lifted a long finger up for emphasis. "I promised a particular ghost we both know that I'd deliver all your family members down to the underground. In return, he did what I requested."

Yeomra drew the long finger beneath his nose like the blade of a knife, and the mu-dang shuddered. She knew Yeomra was behind it, but the memory of her grandson's injury still haunted her. Ultimately, it was her fault.

"Then, do as you must," she said, closing her eyes, but she was only met with silence. Upon reopening them, she saw his narrowed stare upon her.

"You don't seem disturbed by this," he said slowly with distrust. He glared at her for a second more before picking up again. "What are you hiding from me?"

A large toothy grin came to her face, and she looked down at the tea.

"You didn't expect me to go without a fight—even a little one, did you?"

He lowered his head to his cup and ran his tongue over his lips. A worried squint appeared in his eyes. "What did you do?"

She lifted her arm, showing the gauze that wrapped one arm.

"I got a nasty burn retrieving some flowers earlier. Seems like someone didn't want anyone else getting their hands on certain blossoms." She paused, leveling her eyes upon his yellow ones. "So I decided to make my own special brand of tea with one particular bud I was able to procure."

He froze. "You didn't?"

"I did," she said calmly. "It should make your tricks a little harder to pull off."

Fire grew in his eyes.

He howled and swung his arm, tossing all the cups and plates to the floor. "I wanted to end this calmly—in style. I should've known better."

He slammed a fist down on the table, and the knife for the cake slid off the serving plate.

"You know I lost a perfectly good messenger along the way because of your grandson?" he yelled again, pointing at her.

The whole time her smile never faded. She had had the tea as well and so had to answer.

"Of course, I know. Poor Gangnim. He didn't deserve it—didn't deserve you, either, for that matter."

He stared at her as she continued.

"I ran into an old friend while up there, too," she said, trailing off to insinuate the three-legged bird. "From what I hear, you and a friend enjoy some games from time to time. You wouldn't know what that means, would you?"

He scowled at her, but found his mouth moving with the answer to her question.

"Yes, I know," he sneered.

She leaned forward to hear well before asking her next question. She was getting close to something that was bothering her.

"Who is it then? Who is it that's been helping you with this whole thing?" she said, twirling her finger around to mean the problems in her and her grandson's life. There was no way Yeomra could be doing it by himself. That was clear.

He smiled. This was one answer he didn't mind sharing.

"Nok-di-saeng," he lisped, and catching her

surprised looked, added, "Moon-shin, the good old door god has been in on it from the beginning."

He lowered his hand onto the cake knife without taking his eyes off of her.

"He said I should take you out quickly, but for your little trick," he said and nodded briefly to the tea before he thrust the knife forward into the mu-dang's chest. "I'll take my time."

The mu-dang only gasped. She knew it was coming but didn't know it would be this way. It would've been a surprise no matter what. She blinked trying to keep herself aware of her surroundings and set her hands firmly on the table to balance herself.

"I've made sure of things," she wheezed and then felt her strength escape her. With his hand still on the knife, Yeomra watched her slide off it as she dropped beneath the tabletop.

He stood up to stare at her twisting, heaving body. She was still breathing, and he came around the table, kneeling down to see her better.

She reached up, grabbing his jacket collar to draw him closer.

"I didn't just go to the flower garden," she whispered and swallowed hard to catch her voice again. "There's an escape plan in place. He will find his way back."

Yeomra slapped her hand away and immediately began brushing his jacket for wrinkles, inspecting it for blood. Then he stood up without taking his eyes off her.

"Your grandson is already mine," he said confidently. "And once you bleed out, you will be too."

He forced a strong grin onto his face, but the mu-dang just kept staring.

"Are you sure about that?" she said.

His eyes narrowed on her, but his mouth answered involuntarily. "No."

Saying that, he snapped a hand to his mouth and gritted his teeth as it was too late. The mu-dang closed her eyes, relaxed her neck, and let her head sink to the floor.

She had gotten to him. She had pulled one over on the god of death. Everything else was worth it.

He scoffed once more, and then she heard his footsteps march down the hall and disappear. She tried to control her breathing. There was still one more thing she had to do, and the future depended on it.

Part V: The Future

42
A second in time

-Kent-

Kent woke slowly. At first, everything was blurry, and he batted his eyes to focus them. When things did become clear, he realized he was in some sort of cage made of rock bars.

He shook his head, trying to remember what had just happened. For a second, he recalled the large man with a sword entering Chewy's room. He tried getting away from him but fell and then—Kent froze. He remembered the sword plunging through his chest.

He reached down touching his shirt. Nothing. But he cringed, shifting his arm. At least his broken left arm hadn't changed and he leaned against the rock wall carefully to brace himself.

He sat there a while trying to figure out where exactly he was when a strange man came tumbling out of the mist. At first, Kent didn't know what to think of this man so he stayed still, hoping not to be seen. It was a good thing too because soon he noticed this 'man' had no legs, and it moaned to itself.

"He was here. I had him!"

Then it disappeared back into the mist.

Kent got up slowly, more so out of difficulty. It was hard maneuvering with his broken arm. On top of that, it appeared he had broken the cast at some point. He couldn't remember when.

He reached out, testing the bars. They were cold and rough to the touch but he couldn't figure out where the entrance was. Before he had another chance to think about it, a smaller figure broke through the mist. He recognized it instantly. *Chewy!*

He was about to call out to him, but saw the man striding behind Chewy. He looked like the same one that had stabbed him in the chest, and Kent wasn't about to let it happen again. Shuffling back against the wall, he hoped the shadows kept him hidden.

The purple man grabbed one of the stone bars and a small door opened. He shoved Chewy to the floor and said, "He'll see you soon."

Then it drifted off into the mist.

Kent shuddered watching it leave, and then he turned to Chewy. For the first few seconds, neither did anything. Chewy just rolled around on the ground moaning. Eventually, Kent bent down closer to him. If anyone knew something, it had to be Chewy.

Chewy looked up and his face brightened. Kent

had no idea why.

"Finally!" Chewy said.

"Finally what?" Kent looked at him with a scrunched up brow. He knew Chewy was strange, but it seemed as if Chewy were actually happy to be here.

"I know it's been a while," Chewy started, pulling himself to his feet. "But we should be out of here soon."

"What's been a while?" Kent said, still studying ever movement Chewy made. This felt like some elaborate trick, and he slowly eyed the walls around him. Was he still in Chewy's room? Was all of this some sort of witch illusion?

"Me looking for you," Chewy responded, and slowed down to look at Kent in the eyes. This made Kent worry. The stare he got back from Chewy wasn't the normal, confident one he expected. It was filled with confusion.

"How long have you been here?" Chewy asked.

"Only a couple of minutes," he said, tossing a thumb over his shoulder. "I was just in your room, and only about a second ago I woke up over there."

He paused, seeing Chewy's face wrinkled up in thought.

"What's going on?" Kent demanded. His heart was beginning to beat faster, and he didn't want to look weak. Chewy lifted his head to Kent's slowly. He didn't like the look of this.

"You've been gone for a week," Chewy said,

and swallowed hard. "And we kind of lost your body."

My body? This was a trick. Kent looked down patting his shirt and pants with his one good arm. "What are you talking about? My body's right here."

"Not exactly..." Chewy trailed off, and then suddenly his eyes lit up. "But I have an idea."

Chewy darted his head around the small cage as Kent watched on. What did this kid think—he was going to find a trap door or something?

"What are you doing?" he demanded.

Chewy didn't stop searching but responded with short breaths.

"If I can find a door, I think I can connect us back to the upper world." He paused, looking at Kent. "I'll explain everything later. For now, just trust me."

Trust him—the one kid that knew his secret? He wanted to walk up and push Chewy to the ground, but looking down at his body, he realized he had little to back himself up with at this moment. If anything, Chewy might break another one of his bones, if Kent didn't do it himself by accident.

But before either of them could do anything else, Chewy grabbed his head.

"What is it?" Kent said, reaching out, but he was too late.

Chewy fell to the ground, rolling around in pain. His eyes were shut tight, and he gritted his teeth. It looked like someone had just shot a dose of electricity into Chewy's brain.

Kent backed away as it got worse. All he had wanted was to get back to normal, to stop having accidents all the time. He didn't think going over to Chewy's house for help would lead to any of this.

Finally, Chewy stopped bucking around on the ground before his whole body went limp. For a second, Kent thought Chewy was dead but saw the subtle rise and fall of his chest.

He neared him with ease and put a hand on Chewy's shirt. At Kent's touch, Chewy's eyes opened, staring directly up at the ceiling.

"You okay?" Kent asked wearily.

"Yes," Chewy said in monotone. "But I have some bad news."

Kent just stared at him with question marks in his eyes. Things were making less and less sense. Chewy continued.

"I don't know what that just was, but I'm pretty sure it means I've lost all my powers. I can't feel anything anymore."

Kent heard a tinge of fear in Chewy's voice. He wished the normal Chewy were here. After all, this was supposed to be the boy who could escape anything.

Chewy breathed deeply before picking up again. "And without my power, I can't get us out of here."

Chewy sat up and looked at Kent in the face to

say, "You and I—we're stuck here for a while."

"That's right," a voice hissed from the fog. Both boys shot glances toward the darkness. Chewy jumped to his feet, pushing backwards as did Kent to get as close to the back wall as possible.

"You are here now, and this time you won't be getting away so easily," it moaned again.

Kent gawked down at Chewy who seemed equally shocked and afraid. Seeing this, Kent realized this was no trick. All of this was real, and it was beginning to seem very, very dangerous.

Then the voice spoke again, and as it did, a figure with red eyes swooped into view.

"Finally, I get what was promised to me.

43
My Best Friend

-Clint-

Clint stood at the edge of the door bridge. Down in the middle was the dark lump of his best friend's body. Soon he would have to go back this way to his house and step over it. He wasn't looking forward to that, but he needed to do something else first. Chewy's grandmother had promised an explanation.

As soon as he stepped out, he sensed the change. The house seemed open. He stared around Chewy's room for a second, but nothing seemed different. Listening, he heard no sounds, so he closed the door and hit the lever on the side to get out.

"Hello?" he questioned, entering the hall. The sun was almost gone, and only its remnants glowed in the sky out the front bay windows. Clint stepped carefully toward the kitchen, asking again whether or not anyone was there. In the kitchen, he got his answer.

Chewy's mother lay on the floor, a pool of blood encircling her body. Clint stopped moving. He wasn't sure what to do. Calling 911 seemed appropriate, but how was he going to explain all of this? Luckily, he didn't have to worry too long over it.

"Clint," she moaned from the floor.

She was still alive! Clint scrambled down to her, careful to keep within a safe distance of the blood, and so appeared like someone kneeling in prayer.

A weak finger looped into the air toward the table. Clint ran his eyes over the mess. There were broken teacups and spilled tea, cake and other items. And then he figured it out. The flower! She couldn't speak unless she had the translation flower.

He grabbed it, dusting some cake crumbs from it, and slid it behind the mu-dang's ear. She breathed heavily, and Clint could tell she didn't have long. When she began talking, it came out as if in mid-sentence.

"…can't explain all…" Her voice gave out on her, and her eyes bulged for air before picking up where she had started. "…I hoped things would end differently."

Clint's eyes scanned over her as if searching for a magic button to reset everything to the way it was just shortly before. "I…I can get the police. We can get you to the hospital."

She shook her head.

"I've seen enough to know that this is the way for now," she said, licking her lips that had gone white. "With no females left, the spirit passes on. There won't be anything left for Chewy."

She lifted her eyes to his for a second and said, "Did you get him to the bridge?"

Clint nodded emphatically.

"He's in there. He's…dead but fine," he said.

A small smile came to her face. As it was Chewy's mother's face, the smile came with wide eyes and not tiny slits. She started again, mid-thought. "…there will come a time…"

Clint lowered his head as her voice faded out for a second and then returned.

"…in the future, when Chewy is going to need your help."

"Yes, yes," Clint muttered, hoping to push her along faster. The way her face was draining of color told him they didn't have much longer.

"You need to be ready," she whispered.

"I will be. I can have the police and ambulance here anytime you—"

She shook her head in a way that made him feel she was disappointed. "You. It has to be you. I don't know how, but it has always been you."

Clint stopped. His eyes were large upon her. It had always been…him?

She nodded. She was reading his thoughts.

"After my daughter brought Chewy to me, I had dreams," she said, her chest rising and falling in shallower and shallower breaths. "I knew what to do because you were in them. The door god helped me find this place because you were here."

Clint lowered his eyebrows. It was a little much to handle at this moment, and the words weren't making sense as they entered his ears.

"Why me?"

She gulped some last remaining saliva before resuming. "He's going to come back. And until he does, you need these."

She lifted her other hand and opened it above his. Two metal pins dropped out.

Didn't Chewy have these?

She shook her head. "He did…but you need them more. Keep one on you at all times. They'll be looking for you."

Clint quickly slipped them into his pocket and stared around the kitchen. Already, he felt eyes were watching him.

Then Clint turned back to Chewy's grandmother and shook his head. It was one thing to hear all of this voodoo stuff from Chewy, but seeing it first hand was a little overwhelming. Chewy needed to hear this, not him.

"No!" she snapped, "You need to hear this! After I'm gone, put one of them on Chewy's body. They will keep both of you hidden."

Clint was afraid to ask from what. He nodded and watched as her eyelids fluttered slightly.

"You have a quality Hee-chu doesn't have. It will help him get back here," she wheezed.

"Get back here?" Clint said, tossing his head

around at the messy kitchen. "What are you talking about?"

She tried grabbing his arm but failed, dropping it to the blood by her side. For a second, her eyes rolled into her head as she fought against whatever it was trying to drag her away. With her last strength, she pushed her lips open.

"I saw him."

Clint leaned down further. Something inside of him was again afraid to ask. It told him it would only raise more questions than answers. He asked anyway.

"Saw who?"

As her eyelids sank, her last words came out.

"…Chewy…"

Clint focused on her mouth, hoping more would come. But she was gone.

He lifted his head to the empty kitchen. Just a second ago the room felt full and intense. Now, he had never felt more alone in his life. Every beam of sinking sunlight from the living room window seemed to hit the wall in a way that burned into his memory. The dust hanging in these shafts shimmered.

He stood up, blinking. He wondered what would happen next—not to him, but to this house and Chewy's family. He thought of Chewy's father back in Korea. This would devastate him.

But there was still time to fix things, Clint realized. All they needed was a resurrection flower. Then, Chewy's mom would be back, along with Chewy's grandmother. Even Chewy could come back. He knew Gangnim had destroyed the garden, but there had to be one left somewhere.

The mu-dang's words echoed in his head again. Flowers and all of that stuff would come later, and he pushed it from his mind, heading to Chewy's room.

He shut the door, opened it, and looked down the long corridor. His friend's lifeless body still lay in the center. He stared at it with grief.

For others, like Chewy, this part of the mu-dang's plan would be hard. And Clint began to understand what she had meant. Clint had patience, and if he just followed the mu-dang's words, things would be okay.

His duty was to wait.

This was what he was good at.

44
Another Reunion

-Chewy-

"It took him long enough," the ghost hissed, linking his thin, bony fingers around the bars of their cage.

Chewy and Kent stayed against the wall without taking their eyes off it. Occasionally, Chewy shifted his footing and noticed Kent did the same. He realized that despite their disagreement on things—as in Chewy being alive or not—this was, at that moment, not a problem between the two. They were in this together. With his mu-dang abilities gone, they weren't getting out of here, and this meant Chewy was going to have to deal with this ghost one way or another.

"I'm here," Chewy said, putting as much confidence in his voice as possible. "So now what?"

"We have an eternity for that," it moaned, grinning, and then stopped abruptly, staring at Kent like some foreign creature. It wiggled an extended finger at him. "Who is this?"

Chewy shifted his head over in Kent's direction. He noticed Kent's shaking jaw. Obviously, he wasn't enjoying this.

"He's with me," Chewy said, turning back to the ghost's face, and there he saw confusion. What was going on?

"It's not supposed to be him," the ghost snapped. "He was supposed to get that other one."

"Who?" Chewy said, lifting an eyebrow.

The ghost answered with an angry howl, and both boys jumped, gripping the wall more tightly.

"I swear," it said, shaking its head, "he's nothing but tricks and lies."

Chewy smiled. Now he knew what this thing was talking about. Yeomra had gotten the best of him.

"Even the smartest of us gets tricked from time to time," Chewy said, hoping to fuel the specter's anger. He remembered how the last time its rage was a weak spot. He hoped he would be able to exploit it again. "Look, he got us too."

It leered at him, pressing its gaunt face between the bars.

"Don't compare me to the likes of you," it snarled, opening its mouth in disgust as it slid its deep-pocketed eyes over to Kent. "Or this American trash."

Kent tilted his head in Chewy's direction. "He say something about me?"

Chewy went bug-eyed. He hadn't even noticed.

The ghost was speaking in Korean. Kent had no idea what they were talking about.

"He just said that we're not his type," Chewy answered, slipping in an eyeless smile to keep Kent calm.

He turned back to the ghost then, dropping the smile. "American—what's wrong with them?"

Its eyes narrowed on Chewy before answering.

"They're scum. They stole our country from us, and people like you," he said, dangling another thin-boned finger at Chewy, "let them do it. No pride for your country!"

This time Chewy felt a little fire inside. How dare this thing accuse him of being unpatriotic!

"What do you know?" Chewy snapped, stepping closer. "You hunt down little kids to get back at their grandfathers."

"He took everything from me!" it said, thrusting a finger toward the ground. "I deserve this! This is mine!"

"None of this is yours!" Chewy shouted, moving closer. He wasn't acting out of stupid bravery. This came from much deeper. "You've been fooled. Yeomra wants me. You were just a way to make it happen."

The ghost's eyes wrinkled in fear. Chewy could see it thought as much, too.

"I won't be robbed of my revenge!" it howled.

Chewy jerked his head to the side. The ghost was loud, but Chewy had done it for another reason. At that moment, something had come to him. If he was careful, he might just be able to end this curse now.

"Revenge? You're always speaking of how horrible my grandfather is, and yet you've never even told me what he did! For all I know, you're just a big exaggerator," Chewy said, tossing his arms out.

It lowered its head, and its eyes glowed in a blazing red as the rest of its body expanded. Chewy knew he had hit the right spot, and then he felt a tap on his back from Kent. Chewy didn't even think about turning away from the ghost so tilted his ear to mean he was listening.

"Are you sure this is the best thing to do?" Kent whispered.

Chewy never thought he would hear such fear in Kent's voice. He *was* human after all, and Chewy moved his hand behind his back. He waved Kent away to say, "Not now!" and heard Kent shuffle back to the wall.

The ghost gripped higher up on the bars as its body moved outward, filling with anger.

"Alright," it seethed, "you'll see why your family deserves it. And afterwards, I'm coming in there to finish what I should've done to your family ages ago—wipe it out!"

45
A Cause for Revenge

-Seagull-

The north mobilized its troops shortly after getting the official backing from the Soviet Union and Stalin himself. Without an international backer, we would've had no chance.

You have to remember too, at that time, Korea was not yet acknowledged as two separate countries. That only happened recently. With the end of World War II, the U.S.S.R. was to aid our country in its rebuilding efforts, but that swine of a country, America, had to step in and cut us in half.

For this reason, we Northerners wanted nothing more than to reunite our country. After years of mistreatment by the Japanese, we weren't going to settle for the same from the US. But you Southerners didn't understand. You didn't care about our country like we did.

As soon as the go-ahead was issued from Moscow, I joined the first military unit I could.

Our country has a long history of division and reunification. I wanted to be remembered for my part in this one.

I was in the first wave that crossed the dividing line, and I saw our troops quickly swallow up Seoul. We moved so fast that few people knew what was happening. Most didn't even believe that they were now part of the great North Korean unification effort. But the Americans would never allow this, so we needed more help to stop them.

I headed up a small group of soldiers in areas just south of Seoul. Our job was to find able-bodied men to join the good fight. At first, we had recruiting offices at every school, but not as many men were enlisting as we had thought. So, new orders were issued.

I still remember the first day we put these new orders into effect. It was hot and sticky, and we were to go out to change men's minds—to make them see things our way no matter what.

Getting these instructions, I took two of my best officers to the streets with me. Anyone outside became our target, and we spotted one quickly. A short man. Twenty-something.

We followed him to his house and wasted no time kicking in the door. Inside we hit the jackpot. There were three other twenty-something men hiding out. They cowered seeing us, and I yelled, "Your country calls for you! Are you not listening?"

They didn't move but just stared at us, so I

grabbed the closest one by the collar.

"We've been waiting for you up at the school all week," I said and looked deeply into his eyes. "It wasn't your intention to make us wait, was it?"

Before he could answer, I nodded to one of the other men with me, and he kicked over the table, spraying glass all over the floor. The three men jumped and started shaking. I repeated myself.

"You weren't making us wait, correct?"

They bowed their heads in sorrow and said, "Of course not." They were just busy and would come along immediately as to not disappoint us.

I smiled and patted them on the backs as they filed out of the house. We escorted them all the way to the school. We didn't want to risk them getting lost. And soon, I waved goodbye to them as they were led off to the war.

From that day forward, we increased our numbers drastically.

It went on like this for a week or so, until I hit a little burg of a town nestled amongst the mountains. My men and I no longer hunted for men on the street. We just went right up to each house and walked right in. It was in this particular town that I encountered a true defector. I had never seen one like him before.

It was early in the morning, and I had just one other soldier with me. We walked into the third house of the day and found a family eating around a poorly made table.

My God! These people must have had food

stored somewhere. All of them were chubby if not fat—mom, dad, and son. I instantly grabbed their precious boy by his sweaty collar and barked, "You stuff your mouth while your country is dying!"

He looked at me with his bulgy cheeks and swallowed. He didn't seem disturbed, and this did not sit well with me. This family had fed on the fruit of the land—our land—and now wouldn't even raise a finger to defend it!

I threw him to the ground, and as I did so his father stood up. The man was double my size in width but this didn't slow me down. I said, "Why hasn't your son joined the North in their campaign for unification?"

The fat, old guy stared with puzzlement before saying, "We have nothing to do with this."

"You turn your backs on fellow Koreans! You hate your country that much!" I breathed deeply, seething. "Then your country has no use for you!"

I pulled my government issued pistol out and shot him in the thigh. He fell instantly next to his son, and his wife began screaming. I shoved the gun in her face and said, "Stop screaming, or else I'll make you quiet."

She sat down with her mouth shut.

"We are the government. You listen to us," I said, stepping to the son on the ground. I placed the gun behind his chubby ear and forced him back onto his feet. "If you don't follow us or say things against us, then you are betraying your country. There is no place for people like that."

He said nothing. That chubby face of his just stared back at me, and all I wanted to do was to bring my foot down on it. He looked lazy and selfish. The kind of man that would only take from his motherland, and his silence enraged me more, so I shifted my gun above his father's head.

"What do you have to say!?" I bellowed.

Finally, he dropped his head in respect.

"I will go," he said quietly.

I pushed him out of the house into the street. Shortly after leaving, we heard his mother scream again, but we were already heading up toward the camp.

That foolish boy! Twice he tried running off into the alleys and we had to beat his sides to bring him back. He would do anything in his power to avoid helping his country, and I could see in his slouch he'd enjoy a world run by Americans—by foreigners!

My anger imprinted his face into my head. The roundness. Those bulgy cheeks. I would recognize him anywhere. And you'll never guess what happened.

Over a year later, while supervising the inter-camp Olympics, I saw his face again—but can you believe it—this waste of a human being had traded sides! Looking into it, I found that the North Korean unit he had joined was captured, and then he flipped to help the US—our enemy! Traitors like him deserved to die…and that's when your family stepped in, ruining everything.

46
My Grandfather's Keeper

-Su Bin-

Su Bin bit her lip, catching tears in the old man's eyes. He did everything he could to hold them back. Whatever he had to say next was overpowering him, and the last thing Su Bin wanted was to start crying herself. She needed him to finish the story if there was any hope of helping Chewy.

He coughed, closed his eyes tightly to dry them, and upon opening them, continued.

"I couldn't let Jeong go the same way that American soldier had. I promised his mother, and all I heard were her words echoing through my head. So I jumped out there without thinking."

He stopped for a second, chuckling.

"I hear Chewy's the same way. Act, then think. Well, we are definitely family because I dived out there screaming for Seagull to stop. I knew Han Joong wouldn't agree. He was always more careful."

-Joong Bum-

As soon as I was in the dusty yard, Seagull spotted me and ordered that I halt. It was too late at that point. He had seen me, so I didn't slow down and threw myself at him. He was faster and stronger though. He tossed me to the side with ease, laughing at my foolishness.

"This is what the South has to offer," he snorted.

A strange, unknown rage built up inside of me. I had never felt like this before, and on the ground next to me, I felt a large stone at my side, I slid my fingers around it and waited. Despite my anger, I wanted my breath to return. I knew I would need whatever extra energy I could afford.

Glancing up, I saw the hazy image of Han Joong watching the whole scene from beside the barracks. But Seagull saw what I was doing, and, he followed my line of sight over to Han Joong. In that instant, I knew what I had to, and I got back up.

I lunged toward Seagull and was already halfway through my swing by the time he turned back to me. The rock landed smack into his temple, and I toppled to the ground with him.

The sick, smacking sound rang in my ears, and my head spun. Even though I knew what I had done, I had to blink several times before actually understanding it. There was so much blood everywhere it was hard to believe.

Eventually, I looked to Jeong at my feet. He was coughing a bit, staring wide-eyed at me. Even he didn't think I had it in me. He dragged himself over, as his legs were still weak from the torture. He patted me on the chest, thanking me.

I got to my feet and grabbed his hand. It was difficult at first to get him standing. His legs kept collapsing, but soon he regained control of them and stood shakily beside me.

"You good?" I questioned, eyeing the red mark on his throat where Seagull's heel had been.

He nodded, and rubbing his neck, said, "Better…now."

Before we knew it, Han Joong was next to us, extending his arm for Jeong to grab a hold of, but Jeong just pushed it away.

"I got it, I got it. Don't worry," he said and then looked down at Seagull's body in the pool of growing blood. I looked, too. It still felt unreal to me, but I didn't have long to think about it.

"The match is almost done," Han Joong muttered, his voice thick with worry. And then he did something that I never expected. He turned to Jeong, grabbing him by the shoulders and said, "Jeong, it's time you two got out of here."

Seeing their eyes meet, I found it strange. Something communicated between them that went above my head. Maybe, it was the shock of the moment, but I didn't understand. And then Jeong grabbed my arm, dragging me back toward the barracks. He understood.

On Jeong's arm, I yelled to Han Joong, "What do you think you're doing?"

He did nothing but stood there watching us recede into the dust, until finally he must have felt I needed an explanation.

"There are going to be questions," he said, lowering his eyes to Seagull's bloody head. "I'm going to answer them."

That's when it hit me. I realized what Han Joong was planning and I couldn't let this happen. I pushed Jeong aside and ran back to my brother.

Immediately, he grabbed my shoulders. It wasn't until this point that I realized my eyes were filled with tears. He looked into them and spoke.

"Stop and think about it for a second," he said. "I'm strong—much stronger than you. I can survive something like this. I can make it through. Inside, you know that."

I shook my head, trying to wipe the tears away. He raised his voice.

"Yes, you do! And besides, mom would never let me live it down—leaving her precious son behind."

I froze, hearing those words. It felt like he was joking with me. Me—the precious one?

My face must have said as much because his eyebrows uplifted, and he continued. "Don't act like you didn't know. You're clearly her favorite."

"'No, no," I squeaked through my tears. "You're all we've got. You're the family's big chance. With me, we've got nothing."

He smiled. "Maybe, but when it comes to our parents, I'm like Dad—cold and logical. We do what is needed. But you and mom are identical—full of passion. Your hearts are always in the right place, even when it's dangerous to do so."

Saying this he glared down at Seagull again before saying, "I could've never done this."

He brought his eyes back to me, and for a second, his face lit up as if something new had just occurred to him.

"There's something you have to promise me, though, in case anything happens," he said, pausing to make sure I was listening. I nodded and he continued, "She won't like it one bit, but—"

I pushed away from him, knowing what he was going to say. There was no way I was going to allow this to happen.

"No!" I yelled.

"You have to!" he said, and then noticing my blubbering, he softened his voice. "Besides, it's not like she's going to make life any easier for you. In that area, you've got me beat. I have no idea what I'd do with a girl like her, but I have a feeling you do."

He stared directly into my eyes as if revealing a secret both of us already knew, but I didn't want to listen, or at least, didn't want to admit it to myself. The lies we tell ourselves are sometimes the easiest ones to believe.

He patted me on the chest and said, "They'll be here soon."

I patted his chest as well. I think I wanted to feel him one last time before turning to join Jeong who was waiting impatiently.

And it was clear Jeong was glad he no longer had to drag me. He didn't have the strength. We were lucky, too. As soon as we got behind the first barracks, we heard the stomp of boots as soldiers surrounded Han Joong on every side.

From that day on, my life became a thousand times more difficult…

-Su Bin-

His voice trailed off, and Su Bin looked up to his weary face. She wasn't sure what all of this meant or how it was supposed to help Chewy. Before she could say anything, he raised his head.

"But now I know Han Joong's life too became just as difficult, if not worse," he said.

Su Bin's face scrunched up.

"What do you mean?" she asked softly.

"That's why I've been gone. I found out someone was secretly living here," he said, opening his arms to the bleak, old house. "And that person told me something that I needed time to take in. It was too big to believe after all these years."

Su Bin leaned in, pushing him on with a nod.

"Somewhere, here in South Korea, Han Joong is alive," he said, swallowing hard. "It took sixty years, but my brother has finally come home."

47
Betrayal

-Chewy-

The ghost howled, pushing away from the cage.

"For the next sixty years, I lay in a hospital bed, in a coma...and all because I cared about my country?" it said. "All the while, your family grew and prospered for betraying it. How is that fair?"

Chewy sank to the rocky ground. He couldn't understand it either.

He looked back up at the seething face of the ghost beyond the bars. This was Seagull...or whatever was left of him. That was clear. But his story made no sense. How was this the cause of his family's curse?

Chewy batted his eyes, running it over in his head again. By hitting this man in the temple, his grandfather had kept his promise to Jeong's mother to protect her son. Chewy recalled the ruthless gaekgwi he had encountered. It appeared Jeong had died anyway.

But due to his grandpa's actions, Jeong's father

got revenge. If anything, this should have been a plus in their good deeds column. And all of it didn't take into account his grand uncle taking the blame for it all to save his brother from a life of misery. Chewy shook his head. Where in this was his family's wrong doing?

Looking up, he saw the ghost relax. It had been eyeing him the whole time.

"But finally, Yeomra's come through on his end," it smiled. "And you're all mine."

"Not yet," a voice from the shadows muttered.

Being on the ground, Chewy didn't budge, but he saw from the corner of his eye Kent shaking against the wall in reaction to the thin man that came out of the mist.

Chewy had never seen Yeomra before but as the dark god slunk closer, he recognized him. The pictures on the Internet painted him in a more old-fashioned attire. Who knew the god of death kept up with current styles?

The ghost's face twitched in irritation, but Yeomra lifted a hand to calm him.

"This will only take a minute. Then I'll open this cage for you…and he'll be all yours," Yeomra hissed, and then he lowered his head as he turned to Chewy. "We finally meet."

Chewy wrinkled his forehead. Was this guy serious? Yeomra acted as if this was some kind of honored meeting among friends when in only a couple of minutes, he was about to hand Chewy over to a vengeful ghost. Regardless, Chewy got to his feet, and the dark god continued.

"I was hoping after my saja killed your friend, you'd follow him down to us. Make our job easier, but…the problem with plans is they never work out as they should."

Chewy sensed an undertone of anger. Something wasn't right here.

"They don't work out—like what?" Chewy asked.

Yeomra's face twitched as if trying to hold back but answered the question anyway.

"For starters, my saja was supposed to get your disabled friend—that Clint boy—not this thug," he said, extending a gloved finger at Kent. "Somehow my saja got confused. But…I can see why."

Chewy tossed his head back. With the sling and the broken leg, Kent did seem like a viable option for 'disabled.' He turned back to Yeomra who started up again.

"Besides that," he gritted his teeth, "your grandmother had tricks of her own."

"I could've told you that," Chewy said, thinking of the past couple of days alone and the missing pin from his jacket. He had no idea when his grandmother was ever on the level. "What'd she do to you?"

Yeomra squinted as if holding in his anger.

"She robbed me of my fun!" he blasted out before exhaling slowly while brushing the wrinkles out of his suit. "She snuck off to the So-chon Garden. From the smell of her, she must have gotten there shortly after Gangnim lit it up."

The smell of her? Chewy jerked his head. His grandmother had gone to the garden? Things began clicking together in his head as Yeomra continued.

"And thanks to her antics," he swallowed hard, and spoke in an enraged whisper, "I can no longer lie."

Chewy's head flew upward. "You can't lie?"

Yeomra slammed a fist against one of the bars of the cage. "She put it in the tea, the damned witch!"

Chewy smiled. Truth flower tea. He had to hand it to his grandmother. Not many were able to say they got the best of death. And in that moment, he realized his grandmother had done it to help him. Yeomra had to answer every question truthfully, and Chewy had many needing answers.

"This guy here," Chewy said, swinging a hand over to the ghost, "he says this all started when my grandfather attacked him back in the war. But that doesn't make any sense. Why would we be cursed for that?"

"Cursed?" Yeomra said and grinned. Chewy didn't like the look of that, but Yeomra continued. "If that's the way you want to play it."

He cracked his fingers and resumed. "What happened back then is responsible for this all, but it's not the underlying reason. It's what happened afterwards that brought about all the problems you have today."

Chewy opened his mouth to ask another question but found a long finger lifted up with a loud hush from the dark god.

"Before you say another word, I'd like to point out to you that whatever you might ask next will not be as helpful as you wish. In fact, there's only one question you need the answer to."

Chewy scrunched up his face.

"What question is that?" he said without thinking.

Yeomra smiled.

"I'm happy you asked," he said, putting his hand forward as if offering an elaborate present. "What you really need to know is who is behind this all."

Forgetting where he was, Chewy put one foot closer. He didn't even notice that Yeomra no longer seemed upset with the situation.

"Then...who is behind all of it?"

The dark god lifted his head, ruffling the thin moustache above his lips. "That old fool, the door god—he's been in on it from the beginning."

Chewy's eyes widened. The door god? That couldn't be right. He was like Chewy's personal spirit. They were linked somehow.

"That can't be true," Chewy said, but his voice rang with hesitation.

Yeomra put his head against the bars. "Why do you think you can do what you do?"

"No!" Chewy snapped. "He's been helping me

against you. You're the one behind it all!"

Yeomra chuckled. "Oldest trick in the book, really. If you want to hide what you're doing, make sure you have a good scapegoat to draw away everyone's attention."

Chewy shook his head. All this time, he thought he had someone greater on his side, but now, he felt lost.

Finished with his laugh, Yeomra moved away from the bars and bowed.

"Your royal scapegoat, at your service," he said, and standing straight again, he raised a finger. "Though I do prefer 'Yeomra' if you must call me anything."

"You're lying!" Chewy shouted.

"Try me," Yeomra hissed.

Chewy stared at him. He was afraid what the answer might be, but pushed himself on anyways. "Is any of this a lie?"

Yeormra closed his eyes in bliss, and his lips moved beyond his control. "No."

And with that, the dark god turned, leaving. But just as he was about to step into the surrounding vapor, he lifted a casual hand. "Here's a free one for you," he said, staring back at Chewy. "You were right about one thing."

"What?" Chewy said. Already he could barely breathe.

"I'm not entirely a saint," he smiled. "After giving me that wretched tea, I did stab your mom in the chest. She overstepped her bounds, after all."

"You killed her?" Chewy mouthed; however, nobody heard a sound of it. The words died in his throat.

But the shock on Chewy's face was enough. Yeomra grinned and shrugged an "Oops!" before clapping his hands. With that, the door of their cage opened. The ghost had been waiting impatiently behind Yeomra the whole time.

"He's all yours," Yeomra said to the ghost, and then slid off into the mist, leaving them completely alone.

48
One Last Trick

-Chewy-

Chewy shuffled backwards next to Kent who still stood frozen to the wall. Both watched the specter crack its neck, preparing itself for a good time.

"So that didn't go well, I take it," Kent huffed.

Chewy barely nodded. He couldn't get his head around anything Yeomra said. His mom and grandmother were dead? What was he supposed to do without them? Now, his absent mu-dang powers made sense, and he shivered, knowing it all came back to Yeomra.

The ghost stepped into the cage, and both boys stared at it. A creepy, predator-like smile rose on its face.

"Thought about this for so long…I'd have to say, I don't know what exactly to do, but," it shrugged, "I'll figure something out."

Chewy shook his head. Yeomra—it wasn't Yeomra's fault. He had said so himself. The one behind it all was the door god. Chewy had been betrayed, and his insides stung for being so foolish. The door god had never been on his side. It had all been a game.

Chewy glared over at Kent, catching his attention. With a quick shift of his eyes, he told Kent to go for the opposite corner. He was hoping if they split up, it would give them more time, or at least long enough for Chewy to clear his thoughts.

Both boys inched away from each other. With the space between them, the ghost bounced its head back and forth as if deciding who would go first.

And Chewy couldn't get the image of his dying grandmother out of his head. His grandmother—why did his mind keep coming back to her? She was dead—well, dead again. She was tricky like that. Chewy smirked. Even Yeomra had admitted as much.

The ghost paused, seeing Chewy's half grin.

"Still confident, eh?" it asked and showed a hollow smile back.

Chewy froze, and seeing it, the ghost most likely attributed it to fear, but that was far from the truth. Something had come back to Chewy, something Yeomra had said about his grandmother.

She had tricked him—him, the king of tricksters—and she had done it with magical flowers. Yeomra's words flew through his head again. "From the smell of her…" His grandmother smelled like smoke!

The prior Saturday night flashed across his brain. He thought he had smelled smoke, and he wasn't wrong. He just figured it was Gangnim, despite the protection on the house making that impossible. But it was his grandmother! That explained the missing pin as well. She had taken it. And if she had taken that, maybe, she had also left him something.

He began rummaging around in his pockets, and Kent, from his corner, glared at him.

"What are you doing?" Kent said, pointing to the ghost. "I don't think you have anything that's going to stop that!"

Taking stock of what he had, Chewy touched each bag, counting. One, two, three, four, five…six! He turned and glared at Kent who went bug-eyed. He didn't understand, but for Chewy, everything was now coming together. The ghost caught this.

"What are you up to?" it said. "You and your family always up to tricks."

Chewy ignored it. Recounting the flowers he had. He was sure there were only five before: the sleeping flower, the truth flower, the fart flower, the vanishing flower and one untested one. They were in neatly marked and numbered bags—all of them, except one.

He pulled the unmarked bag out and eyed Kent's worried face. "I think we may have a way out of here."

Looking down, he noticed the bag came with a piece of paper. With no time to read, he slid it back into his pocket. Then he looked fully upon the large, looming ghost. Anger and worry had come back to its face. It sensed its prey was doing something it wouldn't like.

"You won't be going anywhere," it snapped as it clasped its long, bony fingers around Chewy's neck.

In that second, pain shot up and down Chewy's spine. It felt like electricity burning him from the inside. He wanted to scream but the ghost's grip was so tight on his throat, no sound was able to escape. He dove his hand with the bag back into his pocket but in that second, the ghost yanked his hand back out and pinned it to the wall.

"This is not the way it's supposed to end," Chewy wheezed, feeling his fingers lose their strength, and watched the bag drop to the ground. Everything started to fade in and out as the ghost cackled in front of him.

"Can you feel it burning in your stomach?" it said, smiling. "Can you feel the blood leaving your feet?"

Trying to fight against it, Chewy closed his eyes and gritted his teeth, but the pain was overwhelming. Tears lined his brightly reddened face. With his eyes shut, Chewy felt the specter's hot breath wash over his face. He could smell the tar of rotting flesh. Chewy wished it was all over but knew that was unlikely. The ghost was going to keep this going for as long as it could. Fortunately, for Chewy, someone else stepped in.

"This was your whole plan?"

Chewy batted his eyes at Kent's voice.

"This stupid bag is it?" Kent squeaked in disbelief.

Behind the ghost, Chewy saw Kent standing by the open door. He looked ready to dart outside into the mist and disappear forever. What did he care about Chewy? But clearly, he didn't want to be down here, wandering around for the rest of eternity. Chewy was his only way out.

But before either could do anything, the ghost spun around toward Kent and the bag.

"So that was your trick," it seethed, dropping Chewy to the ground. "Distract me with my hatred again while you concoct an escape plan. Well, not this time!"

It reached out and grabbed Kent's arm that held the flower bag. The force of it caused Kent's bad leg to buckle, and he dropped to his knees, screaming.

The ghost picked the bag out of Kent's hand delicately as if just touching it was dangerous, and it examined it closely.

"It's one of those flowers Yeomra was talking about, isn't it?" it snarled at teary-eyed Kent. Not getting an answer, it swung back around to Chewy. "Isn't it!"

Chewy tried to look disappointed and lowered

his eyes as if the whole world was coming to an end. The ghost beamed at this.

"Did you really think you'd be able to outsmart me?" it said with a cackle, and then dropped Kent, bringing his other hand up to the bag. "So what's inside? A vanishing flower? A flower that turns living things to stone?"

It turned the bag over in its hand and then paused, squinting at the bag. There was a number three on it.

"What does this mean?" it questioned, drawing one red eye shut.

"It means," Chewy smiled confidently, "you've got the fart flower." And then he drew his other hand out of his pocket. "This here is whatever my grandmother left me, and I have a feeling you're not going to be happy about it."

Chewy turned his palm upside down, pinching the bag's bottom with his fingers to allow the flower to fall out. For a second, everything seemed to move in slow motion as the ghost lunged toward him. Chewy shifted his head to Kent, seeing his pained face disappear as if being erased. There was nothing left of him. Whatever it was worked.

The ghost's hands returned to Chewy's neck as Chewy looked down at his feet. The electricity ran through his spine again, and he saw it—a pink-colored flower. And then…everything went black.

49
My Grandma's Plan

-Chewy-

Chewy's eyes snapped open. The darkness was still around him, so he blinked, hoping it would clear up. He wondered what the flower had done. Had it sucked out all the light from around them?

Turning his head, he realized he was lying on the ground, and as he stretched, his arms banged against a solid wall.

A door bridge!

He sat up, eyeing the dark walls and floor. On both ends, the entrances glowed. He was back...somewhere. Even though it was a door bridge, he didn't know which one or what laid just outside of it, but he was happy to be out of the underground.

He stood up slowly, his body feeling sore and weak. *That's right*, he thought. When he was last inside his body, he had dashed all over town, escaping from Gangnim. And this made him pause. Somewhere, Gangnim was trapped in one of these things, and Chewy shivered, and this brought him to Kent.

Chewy tossed his head around, hoping to see Kent somewhere in the corridor, but getting to his feet, all he found was a pile of trash. On closer inspection, it was filled with Dorito bags and fast food wrappers with what looked like the occasional beer can. Chewy scrunched up his face. There was no way Kent did this.

He shook his head. He would be able to worry about that later. In the meantime, he hoped he still had time to help his mother and grandmother.

Looking at the two ends, he noticed one looked familiar—his bedroom! A rush of excitement filled him. He was home! He was going to see his friends and family again. He had done it!

He darted down the bridge and jumped out with a holler. He was so happy to be back that he wasn't even worried who heard him. But upon exiting, he noticed his room was different.

He went up to the bed, finding the sheets faded and, inspecting the window, he saw grime built up along the pane. The sunlight shining in seemed choked and dingy. Had a dirt bomb gone off in there?

"Mom?" he ventured and stayed quiet for an answer, but nothing came.

He hit the lever on the side of the door, trotted out into the living room, and looked to the kitchen. All the furniture was still there but everything had a layer of dust over an inch thick, and the chairs were shuffled around as if a party of people had just left. Then he spotted it.

On the kitchen floor, an oval-shaped, brown mark disrupted the dusty wood. He gulped. Yeomra was telling the truth.

Worry rose up in Chewy's head, and he looked around frantically. There had to be something he could do, and he dove to the phone hanging on the wall, but the line was dead.

He slid down the wall, frustrated and teary-eyed. He couldn't help but feel this was another of Yeomra's tricks, and this brought him back to the note in his pocket.

He yanked it out and held his breath for a second. This was it. He exhaled and opened the note.

Dear Chewy,

I'm afraid you'll have little time to understand what I have to say, but please know, I did all of this for you.

I'm sorry for disappearing so suddenly. I knew time was limited and I had to act fast. If you knew anything about it, Yeomra would have figured it out. Please understand, I didn't want to do it this way. There are already too many secrets in this family.

First, you've probably already figured out that the saja was supposed to have killed Clint, not Kent. They knew you'd come after him, and that should you ever escape the underground, he'd be there to help you. Death wanted to take away all of your support, but Clint is bound to you in a way you never expected.

This was not Death's only mistake.

During my absence, I was busy. There were two things I had to do under Death's nose. The first was to set up the requirements for you to get out of the underground. I knew, eventually, Yeomra's plan would get you down there. If you are reading this, then it means my hard work has paid off.

The flower this note is attached to is most likely the last resurrection flower in existence. Gangnim didn't lie to you. He burned the garden to the ground. I cannot describe to you what horror it was like to watch, knowing I couldn't help the poor flower warden. I nearly died getting what flowers I could. But the bad news doesn't end there.

After you disappear from seeing this resurrection flower, it will be left in the underground. I don't doubt Yeomra will destroy it as soon he's found you're gone. So be careful! There will be no coming back from now on.

On a lighter note, I've instructed Clint to wait for you. He will tell you everything else you need to know—one of which is the pin in your pocket. Don't lose it! Now that you're in the land of the living again, Yeomra will most likely be searching for you. This pin is the only thing keeping you entirely hidden from him. I only wish I could see his face. In the end, I'll have pulled quite a few over on the god of death, and that brings me to the second part of my plan.

While setting up your escape route, I made precautions to help you find your way back to me. Clint knows nothing of this. At the time, I didn't know if it was in his best interest to know. You know how he worries.

It won't be easy getting back to me. But don't give up. You have everything you need to get it done. Trust me. In the end, everything will make sense, just go back to where it all started.

Love,
Grandma

50
An unusual reunion

-Chewy-

Finished with the letter, Chewy jumped up and ran back to his room.

Of course, Clint!

If there were anyone who could help him figure out what was going on, his best friend would be it. He had always been good at that so far.

Chewy slammed his door, reopened it, and dashed back across the door bridge. Halfway, he spotted the pile of trash again and hopped over it. He hoped Clint had an explanation for that as well.

Getting to the other side, he jumped through the door, fully expecting to see Clint stretched out on the bottom bunk with a worried look on his face. But upon landing, he found the room filled with boxes and trash bags. There seemed to be more of the same garbage here than there was in the bridge.

He stepped carefully through the mess toward Clint's bedroom door when it flew open. Chewy gazed outward, afraid at first that it was Clint's mom. He didn't know how he would explain being in the house at whatever hour of day it was. But that's not what happened.

Instead, a lean, young man with a cane in his right hand stood in the doorway. Looking closer, Chewy saw the man's eyebrows uplift, and was about to ask who he was when the man's mouth fell open in awe.

"You made it! You're finally here," the man said, astonished. He blinked at Chewy as if his eyes were deceiving him.

Chewy drew down his eyebrows. "Who are you exactly?"

The man grinned childishly. "You don't recognize me?" The man scanned his own body as if it was plain to see.

Chewy shook his head. What was this guy talking about?

"It's me, Clint," he piped up with a deep voice.

Chewy's eyes widened. He hadn't noticed it before, but now he saw it: the white hair; the skin that looked like it had barely seen the light of day; even the uncomfortable way he stood. It was his best friend—somehow.

"But your…" Chewy trailed off, looking down at Clint's legs.

Clint looked down as well and smirked.

"My braces? Got them off a while ago. I won't

be racing anytime soon, but as long as I got this guy, I should be fine," he said, lifting up his cane.

"I don't understand," said Chewy, finding his way to an uncluttered chair. He had to sit down. All of this was too much.

"I can explain," Clint started, and even now Chewy began to recognize the tone and pattern of his best friend's voice. "Maybe you don't recall, but your grandmother told us earlier about how time works in levels. The upper realms go slower while the lower reams—the underground—run faster. You remember the tale of Gangnim?"

Chewy stiffened. He did remember. In it, Gangnim went to the underground, and having spent only three hours there, he found upon his return that three years had passed in his absence. Chewy swallowed hard.

"I remember," he whispered, blinking in shock. "How long have I been gone?"

Sticking his tongue out, Clint screwed his eyes up towards the ceiling to do the math before answering.

"I'd have to say about…fifteen years or so," he said, bringing his eyes back down to Chewy's face. "It's been a long time."

Suddenly, everything hit him, and Chewy's eyes started to well up. He wasn't even sure why, but something deep inside him hurt. It was just too much, and he looked up at his best friend's face through watery eyes.

"I'm sorry," he sobbed, wiping his nose on his

sleeve. "If I had just listened to you in the first place, none of this would have happened—like you said."

Clint waved a hand at him. "But you didn't."

Chewy jerked his head. Was Clint reprimanding him? Clint continued.

"Do you remember what you told me about my water-phobia?"

Chewy buckled his shoulders, feeling guilty and nodded.

"You said that my problem was I thought I could wait my problem out, that if I waited long enough, eventually it would go away." He paused, catching Chewy's eye. "In that situation, you were right. Waiting didn't help. But in another situation…"

Clint held his hands out to the room, and Chewy looked around. The bunks were covered in old stuffed animals and clothes, and boxes were lodged in every corner. Besides the mess, the room was practically the same. And Chewy looked up, realizing Clint had waited all these years for him. But Chewy still didn't understand.

Clint smiled at this. "Don't you see? Jumping in to save someone, no matter what—that made you who you are, that made you the Great Chewy Noh. But sometimes, jumping in isn't always the answer."

Chewy lowered his head. He was happy to hear Clint call him 'the Great Chewy Noh' again. And he understood. His strength was also his weakness. He needed to be careful, and he hoped he would be in the future.

"Besides," Clint said, shifting his cane, "what's done is done. There's no changing the past."

Chewy tilted his head, pausing as he heard this. Something in his grandmother's letter clicked in his brain. *Go back to where it all started.*

"Maybe not." Chewy pulled the letter from his pocket and held it up for Clint to see.

"Maybe not," he repeated.

The End

About the Author

I have always loved books. While younger, I read voraciously the classics and experimental forms of narrative. But, more recently, I've backtracked and started enjoying authors like Gaimen, Sachar, and DiCamillo. My writing tends to tackle issues of spirituality, paradigms, and the way we think. My love for reading and writing has only expanded by becoming an English teacher in Korea.

Please leave any comments at my blog: keats0810.wordpress.com

Coming Soon

Chewy Noh and the Legends of Spring

You've never heard of Chewy Noh? Well, at first, when he came, we thought nothing of him. He did well on tests, but so what? Even after his mom got sick, nobody paid attention. That is until the great gym fire.

Afterwards, no one could say for sure it was because of Chewy, but we all thought it. And then kids started getting sick. And the school bully went missing. And finally, a body turned up in his house—his mom's! The strangest thing of all was he was nowhere to be found.

Some say he ran off. Others say he still wanders the night. Either way, for the past fifteen years, his house has sat silent…until now.

So if something strange moans beneath your bed or a shadow slinks out of your closet, don't go looking. It could just be the legend of Chewy Noh—back for revenge!

Other Books by Tim Learn

Chewy Noh
and the Fall of the Mu-dang

Chewy Noh
and the Phantasm of Winter

How to Wear Your Pajamas
(A Squeaker's Brother Journal)

Made in the USA
Charleston, SC
13 January 2016